The Secret
of the
Disappearing
Sultan

The Secret
of the
Disappearing
Sultan

ʒ

MARGERY WARNER

Illustrated by Charles Robinson

1975

Houghton Mifflin Company Boston

Chapter headings are Arabian proverbs.

Library of Congress Cataloging in Publication Data

Warner, Margery.
    The secret of the disappearing sultan.

    SUMMARY: While waiting for her parents to arrive
in Paris, a twelve-year-old American girl becomes an
inadvertent accomplice in trying to save the young sultan of a small Arab state from being abducted by his
enemies.
    [1. Mystery and detective stories. 2. Switzerland—
Fiction] I. Robinson, Charles 1931–   illus.
II. Title.
PZ7.W2456Se   [Fic]   74–33121
ISBN 0-395-20504-2

To Nona

I

"Women are the snares of Satan."

It BEGAN in a hotel in Paris on a day when I woke up with a terrible cold.

I sneezed for about the millionth time and reached for a box of tissues.

"Poor lamb," clucked Mère Benedicte. Her white-robed figure loomed over me, filling nearly all the empty space in that small overfurnished hotel room. She had just taken my temperature and, squinting, held the thermometer to the light.

"No fever," she announced. "Are you sure you won't mind staying here alone today?"

Chantal peered from behind Mère Benedicte.

"If it weren't my last day in Paris I'd stay and play gin rummy with you."

Chantal was a year younger, so I had not known her well at school but she was very sweet. I think she would have stayed, if I had asked her. But that was silly; I didn't mind staying alone.

"I couldn't play rummy," I said. "I would sneeze the cards all over the room!"

Mère Benedicte poured a cup of tea and handed it to me, then plumped the pillows behind my back, tut-tutting quietly all the time and saying I must rest and stay warm. Mère Benedicte was the one the school always sent traveling with the girls. I'm pretty sure because she was always kind and gentle and thoughtful and never, *never* ran out of patience. Which was not something that could be said of all the nuns at that Swiss school!

I convinced them that I would be fine and I was still drinking my tea when they were ready to leave. Teacup in hand I got up and followed them to the door. I could watch them into the elevator and wave goodby. It was a limp wave I gave them but I don't think they noticed because all three of us were staring at the man who stood beside the door to the next room. He was in the long white cloak of an Arab, the scarflike thing over his head held by a black cord. His arms were folded, his brown beaked nose pointed straight ahead, and there was a patch over his eye. I rattled my cup on the saucer — I wanted him to turn so I could see his other eye — but he paid no more attention to me than he had

2

to Mère Benedicte and Chantal as they went down in the elevator. I waited as long as I decently could and then regretfully went back in and shut the door.

I went to stand by the window while I finished my tea. There was a tiny balcony outside the shutters but not the kind one could sit on. And there was nothing much to watch below; mostly I could just see the tops of the trees that lined the street.

Rest and stay warm, Mère Benedicte had said. I flopped on the bed thinking it was going to be a long dull day. Almost as if to contradict me — at least about the dull part — there came the sound of a crashing dish. That was followed immediately by the sound of several loud voices speaking some language I could not understand. A door banged, then another. I went to the door again and looked into the hall. The man with the patch had his back to me and was talking to a tall, elegant-looking man with a small pointed black beard. Unfortunately for my eavesdropping the tall man was looking directly at me. He lifted a hand, apparently to interrupt the other's conversation, and bowed low. To me! I managed an embarrassed smile — I don't mind snooping but I don't like being caught! — and retreated into the room. But not before a door opened farther down the corridor and a third man in Arab robes appeared. It was like a page from the Arabian Nights.

I lay down again and listened intently. Perhaps there would be more entertainment; at least they were colorful neighbors. But nothing happened. There was absolute silence. I finally gave up and scolded myself for not bringing a book. I nearly always take a book when I go anywhere but this time — nothing. I looked over Chantal's bed to see if she had anything to read but nothing was visible there either. So I leaned over and pulled my purse from the top of my suitcase. I would reread my mail, I figured, and then maybe go to sleep.

Not that I had very much mail. A letter and a postcard — that was the total. The letter was from my mother, mailed four days ago, and I stared for a minute at the envelope.

Miss Sarina Thorpe
Institute St. Dominique
Auvernier, Suisse

The letter had arrived at the school the day before we left and mainly went over both our schedules before we got together.

". . . rather pleased that we have been invited to the conference in Bulgaria. It seems they are quite interested in some parts of our work. Then we go to Vienna to see an archeologist there. Then on to Paris a week from Tuesday and nothing but holiday until we leave for home. So hurry, Tuesday! Meantime, you have a nice trip to Paris. I'll write again to the hotel. Love you, Mother."

Maybe there was a letter here already. I reached for the phone and called the desk. There wasn't.

The other piece of mail was from Gordon Danko. He had been a student of my father's a few years ago and had hung around so much that he came to seem like one of the family. Maybe I should say that my father is a professor of archeology. My mother doesn't teach it but she is one — an archeologist — so they travel a lot, digging up old cities and things like that. And since I am the only one, child I mean, I go with them most of the time. A lot of the ladies — especially old ladies — sort of tsk, tsk at me when they hear I'm an Only Child but I don't know anyone *my* age who feels sorry for me. Anyway, since my father's students all seem to adopt us we really have a very large family. Even after they graduate or get married or move away they still belong. Actually that was the worst part of spending a year in that boarding school in Switzerland—not having all those people in and out. That and missing the weddings. For instance, Gordon had just been married.

"We will spend most of the summer traveling around Europe," the card said, "but for the first few weeks we will stay at a friend's house, the Villa Raphael, in the village of Maxewil in Switzerland. We will stop by the school to see you on our way."

But they had not come. So I had not met Gordon's new wife, Betsy. And I was really sorry to have missed their wedding. I lay there, half asleep, thinking of weddings. My favorite so far was the one in a garden where the bride and groom were barefoot and had flowers in their hair and a boy sat on the grass and played the flute.

I think I may have actually fallen asleep when I was startled upright by a series of short, sharp screams and a swirl of angry words. The sounds were coming through the half-open window to the balcony so I poked my head out to listen. The commotion was in the room next door — the Arabian room as I now thought of it.

I slid onto the narrow balcony and sidled along it until I came to the partition that separated it from the neighboring balcony. From there I could see partway into the room.

The only person in sight was a very young hotel maid. She held a tray of dishes in front of her as shield and backed toward the hall door, terror on her face. Whoever was doing the yelling was out of my view, though I leaned forward to try to see.

Suddenly, from behind the drapery of the open window came the swish of a brandished riding quirt and the little maid screamed again. Without thinking what I was doing and feeling furiously indignant I went over the balcony partition and —

I think I ought to say that there is a streak in me that would like to be a heroine. I hate to see fighting. I hate to see things afraid. I have rescued mice from traps. I've rescued birds from cats. I've brought home I can't remember how many stray frightened kittens. And sometimes I forget to be smart because I have also plunged into dogfights and it has been pure luck that I've never been bitten. So this time it was something like a scared kitten *and* a dogfight and without even using my head at all I climbed over the partition and stepped through the open window into the Arabian room.

To my astonishment the person holding the quirt was a boy about my own age — three months older, as it turned out. He looked to be as surprised as I was and while we stared at each other the little maid escaped, leaving the door to fall closed behind her.

"I don't suppose you speak English," I said, "and I don't think my French is good enough to tell you what I think of you. But," I added grimly, "I am going to try!"

" 'Let not your tongue cut your throat,' " said the boy in perfect English. "Instead, I shall tell you what befalls one who enters unbidden into my presence."

"I should approach on my hands and knees, perhaps?"

We glared at each other while he stood at full height. The effect was not very imposing because he had a slightly plump and pudgy quality that I did not find impressive.

"Indeed, there are those who do come on hands and knees — for I am Ta'abata Qabit, the Sultan of Samir!" He pronounced it Tahbahta Kabeet.

"If you treat them as you did that maid I am sorry for the people of Samir!"

"Those who do not obey my commands are punished. She has been told twice to bring me honey!"

"Honey!"

"I cannot eat that pale pink jelly they serve with breakfast. My men told her that yesterday."

I stared at him.

"You mean all that fuss was because you did not have honey for breakfast?" I just shook my head and muttered, "Selfish, spoiled, self-centered — "

"Silence! You may not speak like that to the Sultan of Samir!"

I used my nastiest voice. "Are *you* going to stop me? With that quirt? Just try it, you — you big tub of flab!"

I shocked myself with those words and for a moment I thought I had gone too far and that he really would start hitting me. I think he *did* consider it. But in the end he tossed the quirt onto a chair and said haughtily, "You are not worth my time. 'Women are the snares of Satan!' "

I snorted and turned for the window.

"Wait! Are you an American tourist?" His voice was suddenly so different that I turned to look at him.

"Why?"

"Shansharra, the Regent, who is in charge of my education, tells me that there are more American tourists in Paris than there are Parisians. Are you an American tourist?"

"I am an American."

"Then you must be an American tourist."

"Not exactly."

He stamped his foot impatiently.

"Then what?"

"I am waiting here for my father and mother."

"Are *they* American tourists?"

9

"No. They are archeologists. They have been working in Turkey."

"Why are you here if your parents are in Turkey?"

I shrugged. He was asking too many questions.

"Tell me!" he insisted. And I suddenly thought that I had some questions of my own so I answered his briefly.

"I have been going to a school in Switzerland. I am here for a week waiting for my parents. They had to go to a meeting in Bulgaria on their way from Turkey. Then we are going home."

"But you can't travel alone! No girl can travel all alone!"

I was sorry I couldn't contradict him but I suppose a twelve-year-old girl can't travel alone.

"I am with Mère Benedicte from the school."

He nodded, then asked, "Were you in Switzerland to get an international viewpoint? Shansharra tells me I must have an international viewpoint to rule properly."

I wondered if an international viewpoint included beating maids but it did not seem worth bringing up. I was more interested in the man I had seen in the hall.

"Is there one of your men who has a patch over one eye?" I asked.

"Maruqqish. He is the most faithful of my faithful. But he is not here right now. I don't know where everybody is," he added petulantly.

"Does he really have only one eye — your Maruqqish?"

Ta'abata Qabit, the Sultan of Samir, nodded.

"He lost the other trying to defend my father. He says he would gladly lose his remaining eye defending me," he added complacently.

"It would be a bad trade," I grunted, turning toward the window again.

"You!" he shouted at me. "Why do you talk to me like that? No one else dares to be disrespectful!"

I looked at him over my shoulder.

"When you get your international viewpoint you'll find out that most girls know how to talk to a bully."

He glared at me and I went out through the window to the balcony. As I turned toward my own room the Sultan's door opened and I had a glimpse of three robed figures framed in the doorway. I moved past and was hidden by the draperies at almost the same instant so I was not sure if there were only three of them or if there were more who stood behind. Nor was I sure that they had not seen me. I froze against the glass and tried to move

11

without seeming to move toward my own balcony. I had gone only a few inches though when it was clear that I had not been seen and the conversation became so interesting that I stood still to listen.

One of the men spoke. "Your highness, the heavens have smiled on us. May I speak quickly?"

"All right, Jarjani. What is it?"

"By a miracle of luck and the blessing of Allah we have discovered that Shansharra is plotting betrayal."

"Shansharra? The Regent?" echoed the Sultan. "No. You have made a mistake."

"No, Sire," said Jarjani, his voice sad and apologetic. "No mistake."

"You have misunderstood," repeated the Sultan. "My father selected Shansharra to be Regent for me from all the country. He trusted him. Are you saying that my father misjudged?" he ended fiercely.

"No, no, your highness. It is only that time changes men. There is proof!"

"What proof? Show me!"

A second voice, soft and musical, began.

"Sire — "

"Speak, Zuhir!"

"For your safety you must leave here immediately. You must go to Samir. There you will be protected by your own troops. Once you are aboard the plane there will be time to show you our proof."

"If you are wrong you could be shot, you know! Or possibly beheaded!"

Outside, listening on the balcony, I shook my head in disgust.

Jarjani spoke clearly and earnestly.

"You will be convinced at the airport, Your Highness. If not, the flight may be canceled by your wishes. It is to protect you from danger that we beg you to leave the hotel with us. It is most urgent!"

There was a moment's pause.

"Very well. Prepare my luggage. Maruqqish! Where is that man? Maruqqish!"

"He has been told, Your Highness, of the necessity for speed and is at this moment seeing to the transportation. He will meet us at the airport. Sulafa will pack. Hurry!"

They began opening suitcases, closets, drawers and I resumed the slow edging toward my own balcony. I had just reached the railing when I sneezed. Sometimes you can stop a sneeze or at least feel it coming but this one took me completely by surprise. And not only me! There was an awful moment of silence, then I hurried to get one leg over the partition. But before I could get all the way over I was picked up and put back before the Sultan.

"Who are you?" It was the one they had called Jarjani. He was a lean, handsome man.

The Sultan answered for me.

"That is an American. Not exactly a tourist. I have been asking her questions concerning the international viewpoint."

The three men looked puzzled.

"I don't understand," said Jarjani. "Were you on the balcony — "

I think I was going to say No, but the Sultan answered first.

"She has been there all the time. She left just as you entered, Jarjani."

Jarjani continued to look at me. He spoke at last.

"I am sorry, mademoiselle, that you have stumbled into a very desperate time but nothing is as important as his highness' safety. It would not be safe for you or for us should you stay here to be discovered by Shansharra. Until the Sultan is safe you must remain with us."

II

"He who warms himself at a fire
should know that it burns."

THE MEN were not exactly holding on to me but
they were standing so close beside me that I had the
uncomfortable feeling that if I turned to leave I
would not reach the window. I forced a little laugh.
I've seen people do that in movies but mine did not
come off very well. It was supposed to sound
amused, as if they were all being very foolish — but
as I say, it did not really sound like that at all. But I
tried and with the laugh I said, "I really must go.
My father will be back soon and he will be angry if
I am not in the room." That sounds like a lie —
well, it *was* a lie — but I had been told to say it at
home if someone should telephone or come to the
door when I was alone. So it just sort of came out
without my thinking about it. And of course I had
not thought about His Royal Beastliness.

15

He was standing beside a bowl of fruit and reached for a fig. With his attention apparently on the peeling of it he said lazily, "She is lying. Her father and mother are in Bulgaria and will not come for her for a week. They are archeologists. Both of them. Did you ever hear of a woman scientist? Anyway, she — that girl — is practically alone. Only a nun from the school is staying with her."

I glowered at him. The little tattletale!

"Mère Benedicte will get word to my father though. Besides, no one even knows I have been in your room so how can I be in any danger?"

"You do not know the extent of this plot, mademoiselle. Nor the determination of Shansharra," said another of the men. It was the soft and silklike voice I had heard earlier, that of Zuhir. I was surprised to find that the owner of that voice was a powerful, muscled giant with a badly scarred face.

"But I will go back to my room. I will not say a word to anyone!" I argued.

Zuhir spoke again, very soothingly.

"It will be for a very short time — only until we reach the airport. You'll be home, *insha'allah*, before your nun."

"But — " I began. The Sultan interrupted.

"If my men say you must come, you must come. You were not invited into my room! 'He who warms himself at a fire should know that it burns.'"

"We are wasting precious time," said Jarjani. "Again, I am sorry, mademoiselle, but you must remain with us." He spoke very firmly but softened his words by bowing low before me — twice I had been bowed to in one morning! — and then turned to the third man.

"Sulafa, can you arrange it?"

"With two phone calls and about twenty minutes!" Sulafa was round-faced and cheerful looking.

"Come, mademoiselle. Let us get your things." He looked older than the others but I couldn't be sure. With their heads covered by those scarfs one couldn't tell if a man were bald or gray-haired or what. But he had a large wart on his chin and the three hairs that stood out from that were gray.

"Where is the school you attended, mademoiselle? What is its name?"

I told him and he paused to make a phone call — one of the two he had mentioned, I supposed. It was a quick conversation in a language I didn't understand. I couldn't see how that would arrange things but he seemed satisfied and led me to the balcony. The last view I had of the Sultan, he was

17

picking through the bowl of fruit while Jarjani and Zuhir hurriedly attended to the packing.

In my own room I had finished my suitcase and had begun on the flight bag when I heard Sulafa chuckle softly. I turned to see that he had put Mère Benedicte's white habit over his own robes and was standing before the mirror tying the cord around his ample middle. He caught my eye in the mirror and winked. "We will have a little masquerade!"

"You can't do that!"

"Why not?"

"Well, because — it must be against the law or something." Is it? I never have found out. "Besides, Mère Benedicte wouldn't like it."

"I think she will never know about it. These clothes will be needed for a very short time."

"Why are they needed at all?"

"Think, mademoiselle! Do I want to worry everyone from here all the way to that school you attended and beyond? That would be a foolish thing. This way no one will be alarmed, all will be safe, and *you* will have a tale to tell when you have returned from the airport this afternoon."

"But — "

"Hush! In a few moments I will have complete knowledge of that school of yours — the name of its head, the summer plans, everything. Soon after that the desk clerk will receive a telephone call from the head of your school; he will be told that there has been a small emergency and that a nun will come immediately to take you to your parents. I will make that call; I will come for you. Who will doubt me — a fat respectable nun?"

"But Mère Benedicte will find out when she gets back!"

"If Mère Benedicte returns before you do she will have that message from the head of the school. Will she doubt her own superior? Or a sister nun? Of course not."

"Well, when she *does* find out she won't like it!"

"On the contrary. She would want to insure the safety of the little bird."

"Me being the little bird?"

But he didn't answer. He was rummaging through Mère Benedicte's things looking for the rest of the habit. He had taken off his own hair covering and I saw that he was grizzled gray and thin on top. But when he adjusted Mère Benedicte's headgear — the starched white piece straight across his forehead just above the eyebrows, the other starched piece tight under the chin, and over all the large black scarf — he looked as much a nun as Mère Benedicte. The wart with the three gray hairs added to the impression of a nice plump old nun and even the big black shoes fit in exactly. It was uncanny.

"Shouldn't I have a cross?" he asked, surveying his reflection.

"They usually have one hanging at their waist."

"Let me use yours."

"I don't have one. I'm not a Catholic."

"Then why were you going to a Catholic school?"

"Umm . . . for the international viewpoint."

"Well, I don't think it will be noticed. Here put on your coat. Are you ready? Just these two pieces?"

I nodded. He picked up the suitcase, I took my purse, flight bag and a box of tissues and we went back to the Sultan's room by way of the balcony. Up until that moment it is possible that I could have got away. I could have made a dive for the hall door or lifted the phone and yelled Help! or something. But once we were back in the Sultan's room there was never a chance, though I did argue with them a little.

Jarjani and Zuhir were still packing. Three closed cases stood by the door; two more were open

on the bed. Sultans — this one anyway — apparently did not believe in traveling light.

Sulafa's appearance caused a break in the activity but Sulafa brushed aside their exclamations and there was a short discussion in that language I didn't understand. Sulafa, looking very pleased with himself, turned to me. "My information has come and I am also told that Mère Benedicte is not expected in Switzerland again until school begins in the fall. So until your parents arrive — "

Jarjani interrupted impatiently. "All this is unnecessary. She will be returned as soon as we are safely at the airport." He spoke as if I were an awkward package delivered to the wrong address.

"What time is the car to arrive?"

"In about fifteen minutes."

"I will leave the girl here. I must call the desk from outside. The superior of Mère Benedicte has a message to send."

I sneezed and that reminded me —

"I have a terrible cold," I said. "I'm not supposed to go out of the hotel. And I don't like these tricks on poor Mère Benedicte!"

"Now, now," said Sulafa. "You wouldn't want her to worry about her little bird!"

"I'll stay here and she won't worry. I don't want to go!"

"My life," said the Sultan, "is more important than your cold."

"Not to me!"

"Now who is spoiled and selfish?"

Jarjani spoke. "This has been said before. There is too much to be risked if you stay. You are perfectly safe with us; in fact, you are only safe with us. And you must not argue anymore. Go, Sulafa."

It was an uncomfortable time while Sulafa was gone. Jarjani and Zuhir completed the packing. I sat on the edge of a chair and thought. How could I leave a sign for Mère Benedicte without Shan-sharra finding it. Could I leave crumpled tissues like that fairy-tale character who dropped crumbs to mark a trail?

"Are you sure you are not going to take me to Samir?"

"Certainly," said Jarjani. "Just to the airport. I repeat, if all goes well you will be back before Mère Benedicte. *Insha'allah.*"

"Then I didn't need to pack everything."

"That is in case there is some delay. We wouldn't want someone looking for you too early."

So if I were going to leave crumpled tissues along my trail I did not have to worry about throwing them from a plane! But even though I was thinking about it I wasn't really thinking of doing it, if you know what I mean. But suddenly I thought of an idea that might let someone know I had been here in case something went wrong with their plans. And I didn't think it would reach the attention of Shansharra . . . if I could just manage it. I straightened the pile of flight bag, purse and tissue box on my lap, turning my purse on its side as I did so. Keeping my eyes on the others in the room I slowly slid my mother's letter and the postcard from my purse onto my lap. I waited for a time, unmoving, then pushed them down and out of sight beside the cushion of the chair. I had no idea how often or how well the maids cleaned these rooms but sooner or later someone would know I had been there. That settled, I blew my nose for the fortieth time and prepared for an afternoon's adventure.

Sulafa returned, puffing a little.

"They have been told at the desk that an emergency in the little bird's family has brought another nun to take her away. I am that nun and I have arrived. We will leave immediately."

Jarjani nodded.

"Zuhir, find the luggage truck and take the suitcases down the service elevator. If you are questioned, it is cleaning for the entire staff. His highness and I will descend the service stairs." He bowed to Ta'abata Qabit.

Sulafa guided me toward the elevator. We were alone inside and he said softly, "You may smile or wave to the people at the desk, otherwise say nothing and do not stop walking. I might mention that I carry, under these robes, a very long and very sharp knife."

He did not exactly threaten to use it but I had the feeling that he was capable of many things. If they were protecting me, as they kept saying, of course they had to be prepared for violence. I did as he suggested. I managed a little wave to the desk and kept steadily toward the swinging glass doors. Once outside we went around the corner, down a side street, into an alleyway and past the kitchen door to a waiting car. Zuhir was already there stowing suitcases in the luggage compartment. He took my suitcase from Sulafa and put it in too.

The minute his hands were free, Sulafa took off Mère Benedicte's habit. Like a magician he pulled a hanger from under his own robe and hung the clothes on it. Then he reached into some inner pocket and pulled out a slip of paper with our hotel room number on it and slid that over the top of the hanger. All this he did as fast as if he'd been practicing it! Then he ducked into the hotel. I don't know where he hung it but wherever it was someone would no doubt return it to the room — probably before Mère Benedicte knew it had been taken. He certainly had arranged things!

Zuhir settled himself behind the steering wheel and Sulafa motioned me into the back seat. Jarjani appeared and he and the Sultan climbed in beside me. Sulafa got in front with Zuhir and we started off. I was alone with four robed Arabs.

More and more like the Arabian Nights, I remember thinking. Is that why I was not afraid? I was a little annoyed but I really was not afraid. Not then.

III

*"A strainer is none the worse
for having another hole."*

WE DROVE SLOWLY through the center of Paris. As far as I had been able to see, slowly was the only way one could drive through those crowded streets. The Arabs didn't seem to be worrying about it, however. I thought maybe they would look out the back window to see if they were followed and fuss about speed and act more like desperate men foiling a black and sinister plot. If I were going to be in an adventure I would rather have it seem a little more exciting. Instead it was as if I were on an ordinary trip with some Arab businessmen — unworried, unhurried and as if they knew what they were about. Even His Royal Plumpness sat quietly beside me, his hands in his lap.

I focused on those hands. It was odd. They did not seem to match the rest of him. Where his face was round and soft and rather pale his hands were tight and brown and firm, as if they could do things besides peel figs. I glanced at his face; he was ignoring me.

When we reached the outskirts of town Zuhir drove faster. I remembered that the airport was quite a distance into the countryside so I settled back and looked out the window. We had just come into a stretch bordered by a rather thick forest, looking cool and inviting, when I heard an odd little ping of noise followed by a series of thumps. The car slowed down, bumpily. The others, even the Sultan, seemed to know what had happened and Zuhir was speaking rapidly, a string of words I could not understand. Pretty certainly they were Arabic swearing words — they sounded marvelously furious! Except for that, no one said much of anything, but they all got out and seemed to expect me to as well. I did and then I realized what had happened — a flat tire.

"How long will it take you?" Jarjani asked Zuhir.

"Ten or fifteen minutes," he answered, reaching into the trunk for jack and tools.

"Go, Sulafa. Take His Highness and the girl into the woods, just out of sight of the road."

Sulafa bowed to the Sultan and said to me, "Come, little bird."

I was tired of being called "little bird" but I went.

I was still carrying the things that had been on my lap — the flight bag and my purse and the box of tissues. I hesitated, thinking I might put them back in the car but Sulafa nudged me forward and I went. The Sultan led the way, I followed, and Sulafa came behind. We had taken perhaps twenty steps, far enough to feel really inside the forest when I heard a sound — a really indescribable sound — just behind me. The Sultan and I turned to see Sulafa lying on the ground and stepping around him was the man with the patch over one eye.

"Maruqqish!"

"Aye, Sire." He gave a quick glance over his shoulder and then started forward, both arms spread to shelter us as well as to move us forward.

"Hurry! There is very little time." He pushed us so fast that I had trouble staying on my feet. Once I almost fell and he took the flight bag from me, still urging us deeper into the woods.

"But you — " began the Sultan.

"Hush!" Maruqqish whispered. "In a moment. Hurry."

He herded us deeper into the woods, then angled toward the right. After some minutes we came to a hollow that was edged by a fallen tree. Maruqqish stopped there and sat us down below and behind

29

the tree trunk. He crouched so that his head just topped the log and he could see back along the way we had come.

"Stay here a moment," said Maruqqish softly.

"You were to meet us at the airport," said the Sultan.

"No, no. If they said that they were lying to make you come. They are planning to replace Shansharra with one of their group and take over Samir."

I had had enough. I was tired of plots. I was tired of being in that forest. I was tired of Arabs. I collected my things and started off. I was quite sure I knew where the road lay and if I walked parallel to it I would come out of the woods on the side toward Paris. From there —

I got no further in my plans because I was encircled, lasooed actually, with a red silken cord and hauled back by Maruqqish.

"I cannot let you go," he said simply. "We may need you."

"We do *not* need her!" said His Royal Rudeness. "Let her go, Maruqqish! 'When you get near women you get near trouble.' "

"Your Highness," said Maruqqish hurriedly, "I must insist. I think we may have use for the girl. Will you," he said directly to me, "stay here quietly? Unless you give your word I shall have to tie you to this log."

"Give me the cord," said the Sultan. "I'll tie her. Or I could tie her feet together."

Maruqqish ignored that and went on quickly.

"I must retrace our tracks and set a trail in the other direction to gain a little more time when they discover you are gone. Your answer, mademoiselle?"

Not trusting myself to speak I nodded.

Maruqqish took a knife from the folds of his robe and bowing first, as if to ask permission, cut some threads from the inside seams of the Sultan's robe. With these he started back along the way we had come.

"He is going to put those threads on bushes somewhere to make Jarjani think we have gone the other way," said the Sultan approvingly. "Maruqqish is very clever."

"Which one is telling the truth?" I asked him at last.

"Maruqqish," he answered promptly. "Maruqqish has no reason to lie. The others have their followings. But Maruqqish has no ambition except to serve me. I — I, alone — could have him killed with a word."

I shuddered.

31

"I wish I had never seen you!"

"I did not invite you into my room!"

In a surprisingly short time Maruqqish came into view again. His arms were full of leaves and small branches and he was scattering them as he came, dropping the last of them beside the log.

"Let us go now. We will walk slowly and quietly in this same direction. While I was waiting in the forest for your car I had time to study a map. We are very near a railroad line that leads to Geneva, Switzerland. We will head for that."

"You were waiting for the car?" I asked and at almost the same time the Sultan spoke.

"How did you know it would come that way?"

"Sh!" said Maruqqish. But he explained, speaking softly and in short bursts, as we picked our way through the forest.

"His Highness sent me to buy some honey. When I came back there was a message. I was to wait in a small room near the lobby. His Highness would be down soon, they said. I was restless. I walked back and forth. I went outside and walked in front of the window where I could watch the elevators. From the corner I saw a car full of Arabs and His Highness in the back seat. Very strange, I thought. I borrowed a motorcycle from the cook's assistant."

So. They *should* have looked back to see if they were being followed.

"You mean you followed us dressed like that and no one noticed?"

"I only followed at first. After the first traffic slowdown I was ahead, watching your car in my mirror. After the second turn it was clear that it was heading for the airport."

"And no one saw you? It is impossible!"

Maruqqish grinned modestly.

"There was a rain poncho in the bike bag. It covered me completely. I may have looked unusual but I did not look like an Arab."

"Maruqqish is very clever," said Ta'abata Qabit again, with satisfaction. "I think he also made the flat tire."

"Did you? How?"

"With a bullet."

"I didn't hear a shot!"

"Don't you know about silencers?" asked His Royal Impertinence with a scornful glance.

"I agree that Maruqqish is very clever," I said. "All the more reason that you don't need me. I certainly won't tell anything to those men. I don't even want to see them again!"

"It is not that. We do need you. I have no idea of the extent of the plot or the number of plotters.

There may be many — and all of them would know the Sultan and most of them would recognize me. Only three would recognize you. You will be valuable in buying tickets, keeping watch, many other things perhaps. My duty is primarily to Ta'abata Qabit."

"Mine isn't," I insisted.

Maruqqish shrugged.

"I am sorry, but you must stay. Only to Geneva though. There is a plane for Samir from there and as soon as we are safely on board you will be sent back."

That was familiar — just what the others had said.

"Furthermore," Maruqqish continued, "since you have already left the hotel and no one will worry about you for — what is it? several days? — then if is no worse to go to the airport at Geneva than to go to the airport at Orly as first was planned for you. Is it?"

" 'A strainer is none the worse for having another hole,' " said Ta'abata Qabit.

Before I had a chance to say anything more, Maruqqish said, "Wait now. We are almost at the edge of the woods."

IV

*"There are three states of wretchedness —
sickness, fasting, and travel."*

Wait here," said Maruqqish. He started off but
suddenly turned to look hard at me.

"I'll stay." Maruqqish walked to the edge of the
woods, took a quick look around and was back in
about ten seconds.

"There is the house of a crossing guard a short
distance along the rail line. Come."

Staying within the shelter of the woods we
followed Maruqqish until the house came into view.

"You must go," he said to me, "and ask the
guard to come here. Tell him we want to buy
something from him. If he has a wife, bring her
along too. Hurry!"

I stared at him.

"Hurry! There is not much time. Tell him it is
important."

I started toward the house and after about two steps I began to think. What was to keep me from walking around it and keeping right on going? Going until I found a telephone or a policeman? As if to answer my question, Maruqqish called after me, "Go to that door I can see from here. We will watch you."

I remembered his gun and trudged steadily ahead. I studied the house as I came nearer. It must be something like being a lighthouse keeper, living in these houses at the railroad crossings. Someone had to be there every time a train went by in order to lower the bars across the highway and raise them again when the train had passed. There was a fence with roses climbing over it and behind the fence neat rows of vegetables in the garden. I did not have to go to the door or even inside the garden because a woman was snipping at the roses along the fence. She saw me and watched me come. She was a youngish woman with a plump friendly face, her hair smoothed back from her forehead with a broad black ribbon.

"Please, is your husband at home?" I asked. It was disgusting to have one's voice tremble just asking a simple question.

"Yes, he is here."

"Would you ask him to come — just over there"

36

— I pointed — "and you too, please? It will take just a moment and it is very important."

The woman must have noticed something in my eyes or in the quiver in my voice. At any rate, she asked no questions and went toward her house. She put her head in the door and apparently said something to someone inside, for a moment later a man came out. Both came back, the woman talking softly to the man as they came. Repeating my words, I felt sure.

The man, not much taller than the woman, sharp-eyed and sharp-nosed, said, "Where is it you want us to come? What is it for?"

I answered the first part of the question. "Just there. Just by that tree." I gestured again.

"Who — what — is there?"

"There's a boy and a man. Please come. The man wants to buy something from you."

"Come, Jacques. The child is near tears. But we must stay only a moment. Our baby is asleep and I don't like to leave him alone," she explained.

I led them back along the edge of the woods to the place where Ta'abata Qabit and Maruqqish waited. The woman kept looking at me curiously but the man's eyes were roving the forest warily. Both were astonished to see two Arabs waiting for them.

Maruqqish began at once.

"Thank you for coming. We are in a difficult situation at the moment — too difficult and complex to explain. But it is necessary for me to take these young persons to Geneva hastily and inconspicuously. I would like to buy shirt and trousers of the kind that are commonly worn here. Or I will trade you this robe of mine — it is of finest wool; you see there are many yards of material."

The man looked sharply at the Sultan and me and back again at Maruqqish but the woman took a fold of the material between her fingers and said, "It is good quality. It would make a robe for the baby — or a blanket — and more."

So that was what Maruqqish had planned and why he wanted the wife. She would know good material and want their robes. He *was* clever.

"Do you support his story?" asked the Frenchman of Ta'abata.

"Of course."

"And you?" His eyes searched my face. I hesitated the barest moment and nodded. What good would come of a scene here? And I had to agree that the Arab robes were a danger to us all.

The Frenchman measured Maruqqish with his eyes.

"You are a big man," he said.

"My father's clothes would fit," suggested the woman.

The man nodded.

"And the boy? He will need other clothes too?"

"Not I," said Ta'abata. "I will wear no peasant's clothes."

I snorted or hooted or something and for a moment caught and held Maruqqish's attention. For all that he had only one eye his face could be extraordinarily expressive. In that quick exchange of glances I knew that he saw Ta'abata Qabit exactly as he was — spoiled, selfish, demanding — but loved him anyway. Just as if we had been discussing it, he murmured, "Patience. 'The young raven is beaked like the old.'"

If he meant that the young Sultan was already mean and when he got older he'd be downright dangerous, I would have agreed. I did not think that was Maruqqish's meaning, however. Meantime, he was saying briskly to the French couple, "Will you bring us the clothes then?"

"Come with us to the house. You can change there."

We started forward and I heard Maruqqish behind me, talking to Ta'abata. "Your highness must see that he is endangering himself by appearing as an Arab. You must remove your cloak."

39

"Of course. I have intended to all along. But I shall wear my own clothes."

"Yes, your highness."

Once inside the small house Maruqqish followed the Frenchman through an archway to another room. Ta'abata Qabit untied the silken cord that held his robe and slipped the ropelike circle from around his head. He held the bundle of soft white wool out to the woman.

"Here. You may have this too. It is of finer weave than his."

He was dressed now in slender dark trousers and a white silk shirt. Not exactly what could be seen on every street corner but at least not as conspicuous as the flowing robe. His hair, now uncovered, fell almost to his shoulders, black and curly. There were long-haired boys to be seen around but *that* hair with *those* clothes — well, it was not quite right. I shrugged and hoped they knew what they were doing!

Maruqqish and the Frenchman came back and the transformation was surprising. Maruqqish now wore a pair of baggy gray trousers, a gray shirt and a blue-striped sort of vest sweater. On his head was a beret. From across a street — or through a window on a train — he would attract no particular attention. Except for the eye patch — but I supposed there was nothing that could be done about that. Again, almost as if he were reading my mind, Maruqqish said, "I need a pair of dark glasses. Not too dark. Is there a store nearby? I could send the girl."

"No. There is nothing near. But for the other robe I will give you glasses."

He reached into a bowl on the top shelf of a cupboard and brought down a pair of dark glasses. "These are for bicycle racing; they go around the head."

I expected to be horrified when Maruqqish removed the patch but it was not terrifying — just a closed, somewhat sunken, eye. With the glasses on it was not noticeable at all. Without another thought of his own appearance Maruqqish now spoke to us.

"Monsieur has said that we are in luck; the train for Geneva comes this way in a few minutes and he will signal for a stop. We can buy tickets on board. We will stay quietly here until the train has stopped, then we will quickly board. Please, mademoiselle, will you carry your case and be ready?"

I took the case and he smiled at me. There were some frightening things about Maruqqish — his strength, his one-eyed-look, the way he could drop

41

a man with a single blow, his efficiency with a gun — but there was something reassuring too. I felt, somehow, that I could trust him. I think that is what gave me confidence that things were going to be all right.

There was a warning buzz. Madame went at once to a blackboard that hung on the wall and made a mark. Monsieur said, "The train will pass here in exactly four minutes." He checked his watch and about a minute later he went outside and put a red flag into a holder. "That will stop the train," he said. His wife worked the crank that let bars down across the roadway, stopping highway traffic until the train had passed.

Soon we could hear the rumble of wheels on the track, then a shrill short whistle, then a train slowing. Maruqqish herded Ta'abata and me toward the door and held us there with a gesture. As the train squeaked to a stop the Frenchman crossed the gravel of the roadbed and opened a door to one of the compartments, beckoning to Maruqqish. He helped me in, then the Sultan.

"May the blessing of Allah follow you all the days of your life," said Maruqqish. I smiled and waved at the woman. Ta'abata Qabit settled himself in the corner without a single glance. I made a face at him but he did not see that either. Instead, he was pounding the seat with a frown.

"These seats are hard. And too narrow. And no pillows in the racks. Get the porter!"

"Your Highness. You must be guided by me until we get to Geneva. We must do nothing to attract attention — of porters or conductors or other travelers. But soon I will send the girl for some food."

Maruqqish certainly felt free about sending me on errands but some food would be good. It seemed ages since I had eaten and I had been cold ever since we had sat down in the woods. I shivered and began to cough.

"Hush!" said the Sultan. "You will attract attention!"

I glared at him but as usual he was not looking at me. He was still shifting on the seat as if to get comfortable.

" 'There are three states of wretchedness,' " he grunted, " 'sickness, fasting, and travel.' "

"What are those sayings he keeps using?" I asked.

"Those are Arabian proverbs," Maruqqish said. "We have them for almost all occasions. When people do not read they pass their knowledge by

43

word of mouth. There is even a proverb about proverbs: 'A proverb is to speech what salt is to food.' Much wisdom is pressed into those little sayings."

" 'The threshold weeps forty days when a girl is born,' " murmured Ta'abata.

"We have some proverbs too," I snapped. " 'Pride goeth before a fall!' "

" 'Nothing is as deserving of a long imprisonment as the tongue.' "

I began to cough again as I searched for another

saying—insulting preferably—to top Ta'abata but Maruqqish interposed.

"'Put on the garment of patience' is another small word of advice. Let us all remember that one. And since we need each other, 'Let us not cut down the tree that gives us shade!' For the moment each of us is tree in some measure to the other."

"Some tree," I grumbled, coughing again.

"I need no shelter from any girl," said His Royal Uppityness.

Again Maruqqish smiled at me. We understood about the little monster! I began to enjoy myself and it seemed a good time to discover some answers.

"What is all the plotting about?" I asked. "The others say Shansharra wants to leave the Sultan here and go back alone. You say Jarjani and the others are against Shansharra. What is true?"

"Beneath the truth rests the fact that Samir has changed very little since the beginning of our history. The old Sultan, a very great man, began changes, changes that could bring the country to modern times. This meant that a few men would lose much of their wealth and power. For this reason they bitterly oppose changes. It was these who led the revolt that caused the death of the old Sultan. But it did not end his plans, for he charged

Shansharra with the education of Ta'abata and
with carrying out the modernization of Samir until
the Sultan was old enough to rule. Jarjani and the
others are acting for those who want to prevent
change."

"Why didn't they take over while Shansharra and
the Sultan were away?"

"Ah. Because the people of Samir love their
young Sultan."

"I can't think why," I muttered.

"Maruqqish, you will have her whipped for
insolence!" said the Sultan.

"And," continued Maruqqish, not seeming to
have heard either of us, "unless the Sultan appeared
to support the rulers there would be uprisings. That
is why their story to Ta'abata was so obviously a
lie; Shansharra would never go back *without* the
Sultan no matter what his plans. So the traitors had
to have Ta'abata with them — although I think
they would have kept him almost a prisoner."

"I shall have them all executed," said Ta'abata
fiercely.

"Your Highness might never have known you
were being imprisoned," said Maruqqish. "We
have a proverb for that, too. 'One lie in the Sultan's
head will keep out twenty truths.' "

The Sultan was still fidgeting but it was not an

uncomfortable train at all in spite of his complaining. I liked the small enclosed compartment. It seemed snug and safe.

"We are escaping, aren't we?" I said to Maruqqish. "I saw a movie once where two men were escaping on a train — but they were outside of the train and when it came to a tunnel they had to jump off."

"There must have been many stories of escapes on a train," he said. "And sometimes escapes are made by staying in one place. Do you know the story of Ali Baba? He escaped his enemies by hiding in an enormous jug."

"There was an Australian girl at our school and she told me about someone who got away in a williwaw. That is a sort of small whirlwind that is common in Australia and this man stayed inside it and ran with it — no one could see him."

"That was very clever," said Ta'abata, looking at me for a moment as if he had forgotten that I was a girl or that he was a Sultan or both. "Do you know the story of Ulysses? He escaped in a flock of sheep. He grabbed the wool of the stomach of a sheep and was carried along. No one knew he was there. Though I don't know how he kept his feet up — there is not much space between a sheep and the ground!"

"It makes just riding on a train seem too easy, doesn't it?" I suggested.

"We are not there yet," said Maruqqish, standing to look out the window of the door. "I will feel ready for congratulations only after we have reached that plane."

V

*"He fled from the rain
and sat down under a waterspout."*

SOME TIME LATER — not very long really but by
this time I was so hungry that it seemed forever —
the train slowed down for a station. Maruqqish
gave me a handful of coins.

"As soon as we have stopped," he said, "go to the
kiosk and get bananas, apples, chocolate — anything else that you wish."

"I would prefer a proper meal in the diner," said
His Royal Foolishness.

"You must not leave this compartment until we
get to Geneva," said Maruqqish firmly. It might be
that Ta'abata Qabit could have him destroyed at
will but it did not seem to make Maruqqish fearful.
Another point in favor of that one-eyed man! By
now I really felt that we two were in charge here.

I hopped down the steps and followed directions.

I bought six of everything — two apiece. With my arms full (those little sacks they give you are so flimsy that I had to be careful that I didn't have apples rolling all over the station) and searching for the right door for our compartment I wasn't looking at anything else and I almost bumped into a man who wasn't looking where he was going either. But once I did notice him I stood absolutely rooted to the station floor. I don't think I even breathed. Because, although I had never seen this man before, he was dressed exactly like the other Arabs I had been with earlier. Not only that — he was pausing by each door and looking into the compartments; he was two or three doors from ours. I flew ahead of him and tapped on our door. Maruqqish stood and opened it for me.

"There is an Arab looking into all the windows," I whispered. "Do you think it is one of *them?*"

He sort of puffed up like a frog and nearly filled all the window and part of the door.

"Do not move, Your Highness," he hissed.

He held me lightly in the doorway while he made a long slow business of taking my packages. I think he took out the apples one at a time so that he could keep me there, blocking the doorway.

The Arab gave us a casual glance and passed to the next compartment. Maruqqish's French clothes and my standing there on the steps obviously made a good disguise.

"Did you recognize him?" I asked.

Maruqqish shook his head but he adjusted the blinds downward.

Then we fell on the food and finished every last crumb. Something started me off coughing again and I am afraid I sounded like His Royal Crabbiness when I said, "You know, I was supposed to stay warm and get lots of rest today. Some rest!"

"You should be grateful to have a chance to help the Sultan of Samir," said you-know-who. "Instead all you do is complain!"

I couldn't think of anything really *flattening* to say considering the injustice of that remark so I just snorted. But Maruqqish gave me one of those understanding looks and suggested I stretch out on one of the seats since he was sitting across with the Sultan. So I did. It was quiet for a long time with just the nice joggly railroad sounds to listen to and I tried to think.

I mostly thought about the border and the border guards. After all, I had come along this very railroad line just two days earlier, except going the other way, and I remembered that the customs men had looked at passports. Suppose, I thought, suppose I said to the customs men that I wanted to go to the American Embassy. Suppose I said I was with these Arabs against my wishes. Would Maruqqish shoot them? Or me? I looked at him as he sat staring out the window, his beaky nose looking fierce as ever but his face softened for me by remembering the gentle smile. He would not shoot me; I was sure of that. I didn't think he would shoot the guards. But would it be better to stay with them until Geneva? I did not come to any decision and as it turned out I didn't have to, for I was jolted by the door suddenly swinging open and the Arab I had seen on the station platform burst through.

He bowed to the Sultan, he threw his arms around Maruqqish, all the time talking in a high rapid voice in Arabic. I knew it was Arabic because I heard *insha'allah*'s all the way through. Maruqqish asked several sharp short questions and Ta'abata asked something about Shansharra and then went into a long speech himself, looking very mean. He was probably threatening to hang the villains or take off their heads or something. When they had all settled down I must have looked pretty inquisitive because Maruqqish explained.

"This is the Second Secretary of the Trade Mission in Geneva. He is one of many who have been sent to search for us." Then he introduced me.

The Second Secretary did not seem surprised to see me there; he was so happy to find the Sultan unharmed that he wasn't thinking about anything else. He congratulated Maruqqish over and over again for saving the Sultan and he praised the Sultan over and over again for being so brave. He said nothing about my courageous suffering — in fact, except for changing languages so I could understand him, he didn't seem to notice me at all. After all this praising and congratulating he jumped up again and said that as member of the Trade Mission he had some diplomatic power that could spare us trouble at the border and as we were approaching it now he would go attend to it. He smiled and bowed and sort of glittered at us as he went — all shining teeth and shining eyes and shining brown skin.

I turned to see Maruqqish looking after him thoughtfully and that made me begin to think too.

"Whose side is he on?" I asked. "Are you sure he is on our side? *Your* side, I mean." I changed that because I was still neutral. I rather hoped Maruqqish survived but it would have been pure pleasure to see Ta'abata Qabit suffer.

"I wish I were certain. 'He has an incurable disease who believes all he hears.' "

"Do you mean you think he is lying?" demanded

Ta'abata. "Do you know they used to cut out the tongues of those who lied?"

I ignored that and asked, rather nastily, "What sort of country is Samir where you cannot trust anyone?"

"Better than many!" said Ta'abata.

"Yes," agreed Maruqqish. "For so small a country Samir has made much progress and is watched by its neighbors. When the new ways are settled the opposition will die. *Insha'allah.* And when his highness is grown and can direct the country's development."

That was putting a lot of hope on a pretty skinny stem but I didn't say so and we all retreated into our own thoughts.

Whatever else I came to think about the Second Secretary I have to admit he was good at arranging things. He got us through customs without our so much as seeing an official — so it was a good thing I had not decided to ask for help. He ordered a really royal dinner and had us served in our compartment. He got us off the train and into a taxi so fast that we hardly saw the station. And in less than five minutes he was ushering us into what must be the best hotel in Geneva — right across from the lake, surrounded by gardens and full of marble and mirrors. He said something to the doorman, who saluted and hurried to the hotel desk, while a porter came to lead us to the elevator. Before we got there another bellboy came with the key. The Second Secretary took the key, dismissed the bellboys and got into the elevator with us. Even the elevator was lined with mirrors; they were set in at angles so they reflected in strange directions but what they reflected turned that day upside-down. The doors were closing. I was admiring the elegance of the elevator when I noticed just the thinnest slice of a face in one of those tilted mirrors. I clutched Maruqqish's arm — so hard that he jumped.

I don't know what showed in my face but enough for Maruqqish to put himself between me and the Second Secretary and to bend his head toward me.

"Sulafa!" I whispered. For what I had seen on that strip of reflected face was a wart with three gray hairs. I am not an expert on warts but I would have known that one anywhere. *Anywhere!*

I think Maruqqish must have half expected this; at any rate he did not spend any time figuring out what to do. With a slice of his hand that was so fast I could hardly follow it he struck the Second Secretary on the neck and the Second Secretary just slid to the floor without a sound. To the elevator operator he said, "To the basement! Immediately. Is there any way you can turn out the lights so the elevator cannot be traced?" The elevator boy nodded and snapped a switch. We were in darkness until we reached the basement, a laundry room.

"Which way to the street?" snapped Maruqqish, reaching into his pocket. I think the boy expected a gun or a knife for he shrank against the wall of the elevator. But Maruqqish pulled out a large bill in French francs.

"Here. Take this to the station and get it changed into Swiss francs and have an evening's holiday. Don't come back until tomorrow morning! If you do — " He pointed at the unconscious man on the floor of the elevator. The boy got the point and fled.

Maruqqish opened the first door he saw — it was a storage room — and turned to pick up the Second Secretary. Ta'abata leaned down to help carry the man. The Sultan looked more energetic than I had seen him before and I decided this was his style — putting unconscious bodies in closets.

All this had taken only moments. The outside door was just settling into place after the elevator boy when we went through it ourselves. We were in a short alley; at the end of it there was a spin of automobile traffic and beyond that the glitter of light reflected on the lake. Maruqqish led us that way.

When we reached the corner of the building Maruqqish motioned us to stop, close beside the wall. He studied the traffic, murmured that we should go to the shelter of the trees in the lakeside park across the street.

"Wait till I tell you," he said, sounding just like a school crossing guard at home. But when he took a half step forward he ran right into Jarjani, who came around the corner with a knife in his hand.

Maruqqish was much the stronger and did not have any trouble twisting the knife out of Jarjani's hand and using it against him but while Maruqqish was getting that knife Jarjani reached inside his robes with his other hand and brought it out again, quickly slipping a ring over his finger. I got one good look at that ring. Attached to it but mostly hidden by his hand was a short curved blade about as long as a darning needle. When Maruqqish stabbed him Jarjani fell but as he did so he raked his half-closed hand the length of Maruqqish's thigh. I remember thinking I was going to be sick but I didn't have time because Maruqqish pulled us both into and across the street — brakes squealing, cars swerving all around. By the time we made it into the park, still being pulled by Maruqqish into the shelter of some shrubbery, I didn't know if I was more sick than scared or more scared than sick. So what I did was begin to cry. I said earlier that I had always had a strong yearning to be a heroine. Well, on that night at that moment I had had enough adventure and I didn't want anything to happen to me again. Ever.

I think the Sultan made some remark about the weakness of women but if so I don't remember it. Maruqqish appeared not to notice my tears and was inspecting his leg. There was a long vicious cut that was bleeding badly.

"What do you have in that bag of yours?" he asked. To my surprise I was still carrying my purse and flight bag. I had been carrying it so long it seemed just an extra bulky part of me and it felt funny to put it down.

"I just put in my most f-f-fragile things that I didn't want to get banged around in the plane going home." That brought on a fresh outburst of tears but still Maruqqish ignored them.

"Isn't there anything you could tie around my leg? It will have to be bound tightly if I am to be able to walk."

I have a habit of wrapping things up in other things so as it turned out I did have something he could use. My camera was in a sock and some rocks I had found were in another sock and the music box I had bought as my one important souvenir was rolled up in two scarfs. So I got those things out. The socks he had me hold over the cut and the scarfs he used to bind the leg.

"It must be almost tight enough to stop the circulation," he grunted, "but not quite."

When it satisfied him he stood up and looked at me.

"Someday we will thank you properly, Mademoiselle Sarina," he said softly. "Now we will follow the shore of the lake in this direction while I decide what must be done."

" 'He fled from the rain and sat down under a waterspout,' " commented the Sultan.

VI

"A man should not sleep on silk
until he has walked on sand."

WE WALKED single file, slowly because of the
awkward, stiff-legged gait of Maruqqish. I was
tired and sleepy and empty — as if those tears had
taken more out of me than just a few drops of
saltwater. I wanted someone to turn to — someone
stronger than Maruqqish. Suddenly I asked them,
"Couldn't you call your embassy?"

"Small countries don't have embassies!" said
Ta'abata, scornfully as usual, as if anyone should
have known that.

"We have only the Trade Mission," said Maruqqish, "and I do not know if the First Secretary is of
the same group as the Second Secretary. I cannot
take the chance."

"I have an embassy," I said. "I want to go
there."

"Where is it? Do you know how to get there?"

"It is in Berne. They had a party there once and all the Americans from school went. I think I could get there."

My school was near Geneva — well, two and a half hours by train — and closer than that to Berne. Nearly every Saturday and sometimes Thursday afternoons we took short trips to one city or another. So I had had a lot of experience with the Swiss trains.

"Which is closer? Your school or your embassy?"

"My school, but we can't go to my school; there is nobody there. That's why I had to go to Paris ahead of my parents; they would have come for me at school otherwise. The girls were all sent home and the nuns all go to a camp they run in the summer. So there is nobody there at all — except the farmer who looks after the garden. And he wouldn't know anything about what to do." My voice was rising to a wail and I was pretty close to tears again so I hurried ahead of them and concentrated on not crying. That was how I was first to see the train station. When I saw it I turned and waited for them. By the light from the station I thought Maruqqish was pale and I noticed, too, that there was blood coming through the scarfs around his leg.

"Shouldn't you lie down? Or at least sit so you can put your leg up until it stops bleeding?" I was frightened; I thought he might faint. We have a saying in our family: Don't cry until you have something to cry about. Here I'd been crying already but if Maruqqish passed out I'd really have something to cry about.

He steadied himself against a tree and just stared ahead at the lighted station. I really thought something was the matter with him when he said, "Are they waiting for us there?"

I had some confused idea that he thought he was dying and was talking about angels or whoever Allah sends to collect the faithful but Ta'abata Qabit knew what he meant. He nodded and said, "I have wondered why they haven't followed us. Anyone running could have caught us long ago. Perhaps they *are* ahead and waiting."

I had not given Jarjani's men another thought after the knife fight — but of course Ta'abata and Maruqqish were right. Why hadn't those men followed us? There was a perfectly good reason but we did not know it until much later. It was too bad, too, because we made things a lot harder for ourselves that night by trying to stay hidden. Not only were we anxious to avoid the Samirian plotters but we also thought the police might be after

Maruqqish because of the stabbing. As I think about it now, three years later, we were so clumsy in our movements that night that we should have guessed that no one was looking for us. If they had they must surely have found us. On the other hand maybe Allah has a special fondness for amateurs.

But all of this kind of thinking came later and at that moment we were staring into the lighted space that surrounded the station, wondering if some new danger hid there. As far as we could judge the station was completely deserted.

"If there is a train from here I think you should take it. I cannot go much farther." That was Maruqqish.

"We couldn't leave you here alone!" I said, horrified.

"I would be all right. I will go to the station, I will lie on a bench until I am discovered and taken to a doctor. Not only will my wound be taken care of but I will also serve as decoy while you two go to Berne. To your American Embassy," he said to me.

"Unless those other people find you and kill you!" I was feeling gloomy about everything just then.

"Maruqqish has always said that he would gladly, in fact gratefully, die for me," said the

Sultan, "and I assume he is speaking the truth."

I hated him more at that moment than at any other time before or after but I have wondered since, in view of what he did next, whether he meant that remark quite as it sounded. It may have been that he was simply stating what he knew to be a fact, that appealing to Maruqqish's care for his own safety would not be a useful argument with him. At any rate, I was so disgusted I couldn't find anything to say and it was Ta'abata who went on.

"Stay here," he said. "I am going to look around that station." Maruqqish put out a hand but Ta'abata dodged it easily and said to me, "Where do they list the times for the trains?"

"On a blackboard sort of thing near the door usually," I muttered.

Maruqqish started to say something to stop him but Ta'abata interrupted him.

"I'll be careful. I'll stay in the shadow." And he must have been in deep shadow for I hardly took my eyes off the station and I never did see him.

"Is there anything I can do for you?" I whispered to Maruqqish, who was lying down now. "Would you like my flight case under your head?"

"It would be more useful under my foot, I think. Perhaps that would stop the bleeding."

I arranged it and we stayed silent, looking toward the station. Since waiting always takes longer than anything else you can do, it seemed a very long time that Maruqqish and I were there in the dark together listening and watching. What we heard eventually we could not identify. It was a creaking, rumbling, bumping sound that was odd enough to make Maruqqish struggle to a sitting position. It was coming closer, that strange collection of sounds, but we could see nothing at all until Ta'abata was back with us dragging behind him a two-wheeled wooden cart of some kind. It seemed to make enough noise to bring people from all directions to see what we were doing but no one came. I remember one of the older girls at the school saying that in Switzerland by nine o'clock everyone was off the streets and that in some towns they still rang the curfew bells. I don't know if that is so but it was certainly deserted around us that night — except for a fairly steady lane of auto lights that flickered through the trees.

"There is absolutely no one around that station — no guard, no ticket man, no one," said Ta'abata. "Probably because the next train comes tomorrow morning at eight-seventeen. For Berne. Now," he said to Maruqqish, "please get in the cart and elevate your leg on one of the sides."

"No, no, Your Highness," said Maruqqish, not moving. "I couldn't let you do that."

"Maruqqish! You have been told to obey my orders. This is an order."

Maruqqish sighed and went slowly about the business of hoisting himself up and into the cart. It was about the size of a wheelbarrow so Maruqqish was bent nearly double, with his injured leg sticking up in the air at a sharp angle, but he made it.

Figuring that the idea was to take him to the station I asked, somewhat doubtfully, "Are we going to spend the night in the railroad station?"

"No, no," they both said.

"Too exposed," said Maruqqish.

"But so is this," I argued. "As soon as it begins to get light every passing car will see us."

"That's why we have to leave," said Ta'abata — which made two sentences he had said to me that were not insults! And he added a third — a question.

"You said you had been along this rail line before. What is over there?" He gestured away from the lake.

I had been along there before several times but I certainly did not have any idea what lay out there in the darkness. I didn't even know just where we were!

66

"It seems to me it was mostly farmland with some vineyards and maybe some woodsy sorts of places — I don't know — "

"Let us go and see," he said — as if he were the leader now. And neither Maruqqish nor I said a word against the plan. I helped push the cart to the edge of the trees.

"Go to the street," said Ta'abata to me, "and when you can't see any lights in either direction, let me know."

It took a long time but at last there were no cars coming and Ta'abata rushed the cart forward at my call. It bounced over the curb — I felt a moment's pity for Maruqqish doubled up in it — and together we pushed it across the highway and into a narrow street that led directly away from the lake. We got about a dozen steps into that road before we heard a car go past on the highway behind us. It seemed a triumph.

A moon had risen now and we could see around us to know that we were between fenced fields. We could see a scattering of houses and at the top of a long, gentle slope a dark patch that could only be made by close-growing trees. The minute we saw it we knew it was our destination. I think we were all so tired and so scared by then that the only thing that drove us on was the idea of hiding snugly in a dark shelter. We wanted desperately not to see anyone. Even if someone had offered help I think we would have turned away from it; we would not have felt able to judge if it were a true or false offer. So we struggled up the hill — which did not seem so gentle after about five minutes.

Maruqqish reached for my purse and flight bag; Ta'abata got between the handles of the cart — the first time *he* had ever been anyone's beast of burden — and I pushed with both hands from the back. Since I couldn't see where I was going I just put one foot down and then another. I believe I started counting, which is something I do when I'm involved in something I don't like, and eventually the cart made a turn to the right and came to a stop in the soft dirt beside the road.

We looked into the trees and at least could not see through them to the other side. We were afraid, I was, at least, that it might be just a narrow band of trees, too narrow for shelter. There was a ditch between us and the trees but no fence. Maruqqish had to cross the ditch on his own feet but on the other side he got back in the cart without having to be told. I wondered if he must not enjoy having Ta'abata take care of him for a change.

We stumbled and staggered among the trees and made for the deepest, darkest shadows. I was still

pushing and could see that the faint light along the street behind us was getting dimmer and dimmer. When it seemed to me that it was equally dark on all sides I stopped pushing and stood up with a groan. And by mutual consent, it seemed, we decided to stay just where we were.

We helped Maruqqish onto the ground, where he stretched out, and I put my flight bag under his foot again.

After a moment Maruqqish laughed softly and said, " 'He who takes a cock for a guide has a hencoop for a refuge.' "

It was an apology for having got us stuck out here in an unknown forest but for once Ta'abata and I agreed. Not with him but with each other. We both said, No, it was not Maruqqish's fault.

"Anyway," he added with a sigh, "the two of you together make a good doctor. There seems to be no new bleeding on my leg."

I lay down on one side of Maruqqish and Ta'abata lay on the other. The ground was slightly damp and it did not smell very good — sort of like moldy leaves — and in spite of my coat I was cold. It was miserable. And not only that. No sooner had I put my head down than I started to cough. I coughed and coughed and coughed. Ta'abata sat up and glared at me. I couldn't see him but I knew

70

he was. He was making exaggerated grunts and sighs and generally being unsympathetic. And when I finally stopped coughing I could still hear him muttering and complaining.

"This place is rockier than the shores of Samir!" I heard him say.

Where I was was lumpy but it wasn't rocky so I think he had simply found himself on a stony section. But I didn't bother to tell him.

Mutter, mutter. Then he said, "When I have them arrested I will put them all in a rocky cave and keep them there with bread and water!" There was a pause. "Perhaps not even any bread." Finally he seemed to get settled and went on muttering.

"I know now the meaning of the proverb 'A man should not sleep on silk until he has walked on sand.' I will have that changed to 'until he has slept on the ground.'"

And then we must have all three gone to sleep for we were taken completely by surprise by the man who awakened us.

VII

*"It is better to have bread and an onion with peace
than a stuffed fowl with strife."*

THAT WAS one morning when I woke up instantly.
We all did. We had gone to sleep in the shelter of
the trees with one idea — to be seen by no one. So
to be found lying flat on the ground was unsettling
and frightening and embarrassing all at once. But
the man who stood over us looked more than that.
He looked horrified.

"Mother of all the saints!" he said. "With that
much blood to be lying in these woods! I thought
you all were dead!"

"The bleeding has stopped now," said the Sultan,
inspecting Maruqqish's leg.

"You should see a doctor," said the man.

"We have serious reasons, honorable reasons, for
not wishing to be discovered," said Maruqqish.
"We prefer not to see a doctor." Maruqqish has a

way of saying things that makes you believe him. The stranger believed him now.

"Have you money to pay a doctor if you had not your reasons?"

Nobody answered him right away; it seemed like such a snoopy question. But at last Maruqqish nodded.

The man set his heels together and bowed very slightly.

"I, Marcel Perriard, am not a doctor but I know all the secrets of the woods — which include ways of healing. If you will come to my house I will look at your wound, fix it if I can and tell nobody that I have seen you. For a modest charge."

"Praise be to Allah!" said Maruqqish. "It would be worth a doctor's fee just to wash my leg."

"Praise be to Allah!" echoed the Sultan. " 'The end of night is the beginning of day!' " He gestured Maruqqish into the cart and we took up our positions.

"No, no," said Monsieur Perriard to me. "You carry my baskets. I will push the cart."

One basket seemed to be full of leaves; the other had some small branches, some mushrooms and a jar full of live snails. Ugh.

"Are you collecting these snails? At home we try to get rid of them!" said I.

"They are a delicacy! Did you not know?"

"We eat them at the palace often," said His Royal Loftiness. "But I think they come in cans. Is that so, Maruqqish?"

"Yes. In cans. But I agree they are a great delicacy."

"Bla-aah!" I said, but under my breath.

"It is said that only the rich eat snails. So you see how richly the woods support me," said M. Perriard. "But not so richly as they did."

"What do you mean — the woods support you?" I forget who asked the question but we all wanted to know.

"The forest has treasures. I find them and sell them. Unhappily, the town is growing into the forest. As the forest disappears my treasures are fewer. That is why I cannot entertain you as guests. That is why I can no longer make gifts."

He seemed so sad that I changed the subject back to the treasures.

"But what other treasures — besides snails?"

"I do not often sell the snails. They are tedious to prepare and I do that for my own table. But there are many other things. In one of those baskets under the leaves you will find the most delicate of wild strawberries. Soon there will be raspberries and blackberries. Almost always there

74

are mushrooms. Almost always there are herbs. In the fall there will be nuts. Even in winter there are treasures — green boughs for covering the gardens and decorating the houses, red berries and holly — "

He broke off to tell Ta'abata to take the trail to the right. After the turning we could see a small brown house a short distance away. Coming out from it, like spokes on a wheel, were rows of growing things. I saw mostly vegetables with a few rows of flowers mixed in. It was an inviting house and we entered with pleasure. If yesterday it was the Arabian Nights, today it was Mother Goose!

"Now," said M. Perriard to Maruqqish, "put yourself on that bed."

That bed was almost the only furniture in the room. A table, a few stools, a stove about completed it. But it was still the most interesting room I ever saw. From floor to ceiling were shelves lined with bottles and jars full of leaves and seeds and berries and pods — I could not even guess what they all were — but it made it seem like outside inside.

M. Perriard cleaned Maruqqish's wound while the Sultan and I stood over him. It was an ugly cut, not bleeding anymore but bright red along the edges.

"There is infection starting," said Marcel Perriard. "We are only just in time."

He took one of the largest jars from a shelf and from it he brought a handful of long narrow leaves. He arranged the leaves two or three deep on the cut. Then he pulled a carton from under the bed and took out something blue and white striped — an old shirt, I think — and tore it into strips which he wrapped around the leg, holding the leaves in place.

"There," he said. "In a few days the infection will be gone. Now for your cough." That last was to me — and I had not even noticed that I had been coughing this morning. He poured a small glassful of dark red syrup and handed it to me. I looked at it doubtfully, I guess, because he brought out a branch of tiny berries, so dark a red that they were almost black, and said, "That syrup is nothing but these berries cooked in water with a little honey. Taste it. You will enjoy it. And it is very good for a cough."

He was right. It was delicious. And I don't know if it was that syrup (I never believe commercials!) or what, but I had three glasses of it that morning and never coughed again.

"Now there must be breakfast." He put a loaf of bread and a wedge of cheese on the table. I asked if

I could help and he scooped some berries from his basket into a pan full of holes and sent me outside to wash them. I would see a barrel and a dipper at the corner of the house, he said.

"Please put the cover back carefully," he called after me.

It was rainwater — the only water he had — and I poured several scoops through the berries, letting it run into one of the furrows of his garden, shook the drips off and went back in. The table now had a large pitcher of milk in the middle, a bowl of sugar and three dishes and three spoons. A battered coffee pot was hissing on the stove.

Marcel Perriard cut two thick slices of bread and some cheese and said, "I will take these with me. You two will fix his breakfast" — he nodded toward Maruqqish — "so that he need not come to the table. I must go now to arrive at the marketplace before eight o'clock so — "

"Eight o'clock!" said Ta'abata. "We have to be back at the train station by eight-seventeen!"

"Impossible," said Marcel Perriard. "This man must not walk on that leg until the infection is gone. If he is active before that time the infection may spread — it is possible that the leg would be lost."

"No, no," said Maruqqish. "I am very strong. I do not need to lie down to fight the infection."

"You are a doctor, then?" asked M. Perriard.

"But neither are you," said Ta'abata, though he said it almost as a question, not in the sarcastic tone he usually used with me.

"No," said M. Perriard. "I told you. I am no doctor but I *know* about these things. He must not be moved."

"We thank you but — " began Maruqqish. Ta'abata interrupted him.

"If we have money for lodging will you keep him here?" Again, Ta'abata's voice was mild; he just wanted to know.

"But, Your — " Maruqqish began but stopped himself before he said "Your Highness." We had not talked about it but clearly none of us wanted to try to explain why a real sultan was wandering around Switzerland trying not to be seen.

Marcel Perriard was filling baskets and on top of one he put a small portable scale and the bread and cheese he had cut.

"I am ready now. I must get there in time for the mushroom certificate."

"Mushroom certificate?"

"Yes. There is an expert on mushrooms — of course, I, too, am an expert on mushrooms — but this is an *official* expert and he will give me a paper that says all my mushrooms are edible. I must have it before I can sell them. That way the shoppers know they are not buying poisonous ones. But I have not very much to sell this morning; I should be home in a few hours. When I come we will make arrangements and I will look at the wound again."

He went out the door and Ta'abata went after him.

"I will walk with you part way," I heard him say.

He must not have gone far for I had time only to pour Maruqqish a cup of coffee and put sugar on the berries when Ta'abata returned and we all ate breakfast.

I have had chocolate waffles and blueberry pancakes and fancy sweet rolls but I have *never* had a better breakfast than that one. Those tiny little strawberries! For a time we were too busy to talk. Finally the Sultan said, "I have been thinking."

I gave him a look of astonishment but he pretended not to see it and went on.

"Do you remember how easy it was to be seen on the train? I believe it would be safer to go another way. Monsieur Perriard told me that there is a public trail almost all the way to Berne — close enough so that we could get on a local bus for the rest of the distance. No one will be watching the local buses, do you not agree?"

"A trail? A *walking* trail?" It didn't seem possible to walk all the way to Berne.

"He said it was less than a day's walk."

"And Maruqqish would stay here?"

"I think so. Until we return for him. Your embassy will no doubt send us in a car."

Maruqqish thought it was the best plan under the circumstances since Ta'abata had decided that Maruqqish had to stay until his leg was better.

Nobody asked me but I did have some thoughts of my own and I told them: "I agree to the walk — but on one condition. If we are going to walk on the local trails and ride the local buses Ta'abata has to look more local too."

"How?"

"First he has to have shorter hair."

"Oh, no — "

"I told you before. It is the wrong length — *nobody* has hair like that and you really stand out. If it were just a little shorter you would look just like all the other Swiss boys — except for your shirt."

"What's the matter with my shirt?"

"It is a very nice shirt, actually," I said, enjoying this, "but it is not quite right. You need something more — well — more ordinary. Silk shirts are not ordinary. By the way, are you still opposed to wearing peasant clothes?"

He seemed to think for a moment, then shook his head.

"No. That seems very unimportant."

"Then perhaps M. Perriard has something he will sell you."

I rummaged in my flight case and brought out a pair of nail scissors.

"Shall I?" I asked.

"Is it necessary?" Ta'abata asked of Maruqqish and Maruqqish nodded.

"Consider it a disguise for the sake of safety," Maruqqish said as consolation.

Ta'abata grunted and sat on a stool. The scissors were so small that it took a long time and I did a terrible job but fortunately his hair was curly enough so that it didn't show how uneven it was. During the whole time he kept up a muttering of things I couldn't understand but I thought of them as black Arabic oaths and I still think they were. Maruqqish was trying not to laugh and I was having a thoroughly good time for the first time since — since when? Yesterday? It didn't seem possible. I should add that I was right about his hair. When I finished he really didn't look foreign

anymore — I mean he could have passed for a Swiss boy easily.

There was a small mirror on the wall and Ta'abata looked at himself and grunted again. He didn't thank me — he did not say anything to me actually — and he slid a stool near Maruqqish's bed and sat down beside him.

"Do you remember that you once tried to teach me a sort of self-defense?"

Maruqqish nodded.

"Was that the manner in which you made Sulafa unconscious? And the Second Secretary?"

Again Maruqqish nodded.

"I am sorry I did not listen," said the Sultan. "You should have made me listen." (I tried to imagine someone *making* him do anything!) "Will you begin again? Is there something you could show me while you are lying there?"

"I can show you the points on the body which are sensitive to pressure. If you know them well and strike them with a sudden sharp blow with the side of the hand it is possible to immobilize a person — even someone much larger than you."

He went over the spots one by one, showing how the nerves could be numbed by a blow. I listened too. You never know when you might need something like that. At least that was how I felt that morning. And we stayed with it until Marcel Perriard returned.

He brought bread and milk and some other things but before he even got them unloaded on to the table we began making arrangements. Maruqqish would be welcome there until his leg had improved.

"How will you sleep if I stay on your bed?" asked Maruqqish.

"Ah! There is only one bed but there are two mattresses! And though you will have but simple food you will be well cared for."

" 'It is better to have bread and an onion with peace than a stuffed fowl with strife,' " said Maruqqish gratefully.

They agreed on a price for his staying there but I noticed that Maruqqish had to convince him to take more than he'd asked for.

Marcel Perriard found an old black turtleneck sweater — hand-knit by his sister, he said — and traded it to Ta'abata for his silk shirt. That sweater really turned Ta'abata into a local boy.

While at the marketplace that morning M. Perriard had looked up the address of the United States Embassy and had even found the number of the right bus for us to take when we got to Berne. He cut us some bread and cheese and put it in a paper sack — in case we should get hungry along the way.

Maruqqish gave Ta'abata a fat stack of French money.

"You must get this changed into Swiss francs at the first bank you come to," he said, "and you may prefer to take a taxi once you get to Berne."

I still had my allowance from school in Swiss francs so money was not one of our problems. Actually, we didn't feel we had any problems that morning. We were going to Berne in the safest possible way. We were going directly to the embassy where they would take care of everything.

We repeated that we would come for Maruqqish as soon as they were able to send a car.

As we started out the door Ta'abata saw the cart he had taken from the railroad station and said, "Monsieur Perriard, will you return this cart to the station someday when you are not too busy? Maruqqish will pay you for your time; I know your days are very full."

I stared at the Sultan — with my mouth open, I imagine — and then looked at Maruqqish to see if he was noticing how much Ta'abata had changed overnight. Personally, I could hardly believe what I heard but Maruqqish just looked satisfied and wished us well.

"We will meet again soon. *Insha'allah.*"

Speaking of things I could hardly believe, I was not convinced we could walk all the way to Berne and get there that same day. If I am ever to find out, though, I will have to go back to Switzerland and try it all over again. Because as it turned out we walked only part of the way.

VIII

*"The mouse that has but one hole
is soon caught."*

Monsieur Perriard walked with us to the edge
of the wood and showed us the first of the yellow
trail signs that we must follow. If we watched for
them we could not possibly get lost, he said, and
there was nothing that could happen to us; we
would be close to settlements of one sort and
another all the way.

We thanked him and started off but he called
after us, "Do you speak German?"

Neither of us did.

"You will pass from the French-speaking section
into the German-speaking section before you arrive. But in Berne they speak all languages, even
English, so you will have no trouble." He waved
and was gone.

It was a beautiful day and the trail led off across

some fields and around the edge of a hill. I felt very cheerful — not like the night before — and was thinking that now that it was nearly over I was glad it had all come about. I would hate to have missed Marcel Perriard and his house in the woods. I would always remember Maruqqish and the Sultan. I still didn't *like* the Sultan but he was interesting to know. At about that point he broke into all those satisfied thoughts.

"What part of the United States do you come from?"

"California."

"What did you say your name was? Sarina?"

"Sarina Thorpe."

"Sarina, would you say that most girls from the United States are like you?"

"Ta'abata," I mimicked, "would you say that most sultans are like you?"

He frowned and shook his head, as if to shake my question away, and went on with his own idea.

"Because, you see, you are very different from the girls in Samir."

"How am I different?"

"Oof! Just about every way I can think of! You will talk to anyone as if you are not a bit shy or afraid. You were even *impudent* to me. You know a foreign language. You know your way around these Swiss trains. You have ideas. Samirian girls just look at the ground and giggle."

"Maybe it is because of the way they are treated. I mean, you have all those proverbs about women being the snares of Satan and things like that."

He seemed impressed by that thought and was silent for a time. Then he said, "That might be so. You know it was not long ago that most girl babies were put out to die." He gave me a funny sideways look as if he expected me to explode at that idea but I didn't and he went on, "There is another proverb: 'The female is of all animals the better save only in mankind.'"

"Yes. That's it. So they are probably taught to be quiet and not bother anyone or think for themselves. Do they go to school?"

"I don't know. I don't think so. We do not have many schools in Samir. Mostly tutors come in to teach."

"I think if everybody went to school together the girls would learn to have ideas and speak out about them. Of course all the girls at home wouldn't speak French and know about Swiss trains — I just happen to have been here all last year."

"But you do know about things. I think it must

89

be the schools. Thank you. That is a good addition to my international viewpoint."

That made me smile but I pretended to be looking at some flowers at the edge of the trail so that he couldn't see my face. And at what he said next I had to stare at those flowers harder than ever or I really would have laughed.

"At home my friends call me Ta'ab. *They* are all boys, of course, but you may call me that too." It was as if he were turning me into a princess or some other honorary state! But in spite of myself I was pleased.

We had walked a couple of hours — long enough to have been hungry for our bread and cheese — and the trail had climbed a rather long hill and then turned to follow the edge of a ravine. At the bottom of the ravine was a stream that appeared and disappeared between the bushes. I walked with my eyes on the stream and almost stumbled over a rolled-up sleeping bag. It and a coat and a guitar case had been piled by the side of the trail but there was no one in sight as far as we could see.

The moment Ta'ab spotted the guitar case he flopped on the grass beside it.

"We need a short rest," he said, reaching for the case.

"What are you doing? The owner of these things is probably right around somewhere. Maybe he went down to the stream for a drink."

"Probably so," said Ta'abata, taking out the guitar. "He certainly won't mind if I look at his guitar."

I shrugged and sat down some distance away — to indicate that I had had nothing to do with the guitar — but after Ta'ab began to play I had to come a little closer to listen and to watch. The tune he made was different from anything I had ever heard — strange and mysterious and a little sad. Again I noticed his hands — quick and firm as he played. We were both so engrossed, he playing, I listening, that we didn't see a figure climbing the hill from the stream until he was nearly up to the trail. It was a young man with long hair and a battered old hat on his head.

I would have jumped up and apologized but Ta'ab, when he finally saw him, just sat there and when the man was close enough said, "This is not a bad guitar. The E string is frayed though; it will break soon." Then he casually reached for the case as if he were going to put it away.

"No, wait!" said the young man. "What were you playing? That wonderful song — what was it?"

"It is a folk song of my country. It is Arabian."

"Will you teach it to me? Are there more like that? I love those minor, melancholy keys!"

"I could teach you easily," said Ta'ab, "but we have a long way to go, I think."

"Where are you going?"

"To Berne. And we must be there this afternoon."

The young man sat down and reached for the guitar.

"In that case you'll have time to teach me all the songs you know! I have a camper-bus parked not far from here and I can drive you to Berne in about half an hour. How is that?"

How was that? That was wonderful!

"Stay here then!" said the young man, bouncing up again. "I'll be right back!" He rushed off and, a few minutes later, rushed back, breathless. He had with him a small portable tape recorder.

We sat down in a tight little knot and Ta'ab played and sang and the man recorded. In between times we talked a little, too. The young man was from Ireland, his name was Michael O'Duffy, he was twenty-two years old, he was spending the summer roaming across Europe and when he needed money he played his guitar in cafés or on street corners.

"I haven't been doing very well with the songs

lately though," he said, "because there is someone playing a guitar on nearly every street corner and town square and riverbank on the whole continent! But I've never heard any like these. Maybe they'll change my luck!"

When Ta'ab stopped he must have had eight or ten songs recorded. Then they went over them and wrote down chords and keys for them.

"Now," said Michael O'Duffy, getting up and stretching, "it is on to Berne."

He picked up his gear and led off down the trail. After a bit he turned, with us right behind him, climbed a small hill and there, in a little parking lot, was his bus.

"Hop in," he said, throwing his bag into the back.

So, in spite of the songs — or maybe because of the songs — we had saved a lot of time and reached the United States Embassy early in the afternoon. We said goodby and thanks and have a good trip and all those things — we had met some of the *nicest* people! — and I was feeling really triumphant. I remember I sort of danced up the steps and Ta'ab must have been feeling as excited as I was because he said, " 'On the day of victory, no fatigue is felt!' " I agreed. I could have run all the way back to M. Perriard's house.

We pushed open the door together and were in a big room with some chairs and potted plants and a desk in one corner — empty. A door at one side opened and a young man entered and smiled at us. He had a folder in his hands and went to the desk.

"Good afternoon," he said.

"Good afternoon. We would like to see the Ambassador, please," I said.

"The Ambassador is in Italy," he said.

"Is there a Vice-Ambassador?"

"There is an Undersecretary but he went to the same conference in Italy. We are awfully short of people right now. Even Miss Blake — she's the receptionist who usually sits here — is home, ill. But I am the Junior Secretary. Maybe I can help you."

"Well — " I looked at Ta'ab and he shrugged and so I stumbled into my story. This was the Sultan of Samir and I was an American citizen and we needed to stay here until we could get in touch with my parents and the Regent of Samir.

Where were they?

Well, the Regent was in Paris yesterday; we did not know if he was still there or not. My parents were in Bulgaria. I didn't know just where.

He looked very doubtful and seemed to back

away from us and, thinking it over, I can see why. It was quite a story.

"What is it you want us to do?"

"I thought you'd *know* what to do. And we can stay here while you do it."

"You know, you can't just stay *here*."

"Why not?"

"We don't put people up as if we ran a hotel!"

"But I've heard of people going to the United States Embassy when they needed to be safe."

"Well—yes—sometimes we do give asylum—"

"Asylum! That's it. His Royal Highness needs asylum. And I guess I do, too. Anyway, I need to be someplace safe."

We both tried to explain why we needed to be safe but it was clear that the Junior Secretary did not know what to make of us and our story. And also that he didn't know what to do with us.

"If you give me some time," he said, "an hour or so, I will see what I can find out. But I should warn you — if you have your facts right — that we very rarely can interfere with the internal affairs of another country."

"But — "

"Never mind that now though. Come back later and I'll see what I can do."

Well, it had not gone the way I had expected at

all — not at *all*. I thought as soon as we reached the embassy there would be lots of people scurrying around to get a car — we had not even mentioned Maruqqish — and making international phone calls and showing us to our rooms and offering to send out for lunch and things like that. Instead of that we seemed to know more about what ought to be done than they did.

We wondered what the Junior Secretary would do while we were gone. Ta'ab thought he'd call the Ambassador in Italy but I rather thought he'd look in a book and find out what he was supposed to do. We both hoped it would be all straightened out when we got back. So in the meantime there were two things I wanted to show Ta'ab in Berne and on the way we could get his money changed into Swiss francs.

We came to a bank in just a few blocks and getting the money changed took about a minute. At home in the town where I live I don't think you could go into the first bank you came to and get foreign money changed — maybe you could but I think you'd have to go downtown — but in Switzerland you can do it anywhere. (My aunts used to put dollar bills in their letters when they wrote me at school so I was used to getting money changed into Swiss francs.) And another good thing for us was that in Switzerland there are so many languages spoken — especially in the capital, Berne — that nobody noticed that we spoke English half the time or that we spoke French with a foreign accent. In fact, there are a lot of people on the streets of Berne in their native clothes so that even if Ta'ab had been wearing his robes he wouldn't have attracted much attention in that city.

Soon after the bank we came to an open market. I'd seen them selling vegetables on the street lots of times but this was like a giant bake sale with bread and cookies and tarts and candied nuts and cotton candy. We bought a sample of just about everything we saw and took it to a little park which was one of the things I wanted to show Ta'ab.

The park was next to the capitol building — one of the places my school class visited — and the thing I loved about it was the duck pond. It was cool and ferny with a waterfall at one side and rocks and flowers around the edges. At least a dozen different kinds of ducks lived there. We sat on the stones and ate all those things we had bought — with a little help from the ducks.

"Where are the beggars?" asked Ta'ab suddenly.

"What beggars?" That was a stupid thing to say but I really did not know what he was talking about.

"The poor people. The people who live by begging."

"I don't think there are any."

"There must be. All countries have beggars."

"I've never seen any. My father said once that everyone had a job in Switzerland — could that be the reason?"

"Begging is sort of a job," he said.

"Not a very good one!"

"No. Not a very good one. I must ask Shansharra about this." He was building the international viewpoint again, I supposed. All the same, I admired the way he kept asking about things. I would never have thought about beggars.

"Come on," I said after a while. "I have something else to show you."

It was about a five-minute walk and I took him on a guided tour down the main street, Marktgasse. I showed him the clock where creatures march around beating drums on the hour. I showed him the flags with the bears on them.

"Did you know that Berne is named for bears?" I asked. "That's why they have a bear on the flag.

And I guess that's why they have what I'm going to show you next."

We crossed a bridge and turned into an enclosure that held three bear pits and inside were some of the sleekest, smartest bears in the world. There were signs telling what the bears could *not* eat but there was also a kiosk selling packages of things that the bears could eat. I bought a package of apples and carrots and Ta'ab bought a sack of special cookies and we joined the other people hanging over the cement railings.

The bears did somersaults and clapped hands and stood on their heads and wiggled their feet and the more the people laughed and clapped the more the bears seemed to enjoy their tricks.

"There are your beggars!" I said.

"That's the best kind!"

It didn't seem one could ever get tired of watching them but I dragged Ta'ab around to the third pit, the one at the back, because that is where the baby bears are kept. They were too young to do tricks but they were just as much fun to watch. They climbed poles and swung on a tire and chased each other and drank from bottles — I loved watching those babies and so did Ta'ab. In fact, it was when we were watching them that Ta'ab said,

"Maybe it would be best if you went back to the embassy alone."

I couldn't imagine why and I didn't like that idea at all.

"You just want to stay and watch the bears!" I accused him.

He turned and looked at me straight on and said, in the most serious tone I'd ever heard him use, "No, Sarina. That is not it. I have a feeling — I can't explain it — but wouldn't it be safer if I stayed? And if they are going to help us you could come and get me. But if something is wrong — " His voice trailed off. " 'The mouse that has but one hole is soon caught,' " he added.

I couldn't see what that had to do with it; I thought he was just making excuses so he could stay and enjoy himself.

"You could be discovered here just as well," I argued.

"Nobody could see me here! This is totally sheltered back here!"

Yes, if he stayed back there I supposed that was true. I shrugged and agreed to go alone. I was pretty disgusted and muttered to myself that I had been wrong to think he had changed, that he was just as selfish as ever. And probably a coward besides. And why should I have to walk all that

100

way by myself. And so on. Which was why when I saw a bus labeled with the name of the street the embassy was on I got on it.

I perched near the door watching for the time to get off. When I saw the American flag flying ahead I stood up and the bus slowed for the stop. I had my foot on the bottom step and was about to jump down when I found myself looking straight into the eyes of Sulafa!

IX

"Fear teaches how to run."

I BACKED RIGHT UP into the bus again, bumping into a woman behind me. In the confusion I shook my head violently at the driver and pointed vaguely ahead, trying to show that I had made a mistake in my stop.

It had been a mistake, all right, for Sulafa had been at the wheel of a green car parked on a side street that looked directly at the American Embassy and at all the traffic that went in front of it. I know he recognized me — we looked straight at one another. I had the impression that there were others in the car but I hadn't seen their faces and I couldn't have said how many.

I waited two stops to see if the green car was following. It wasn't, as far as I could see. Then I saw a bus coming the other direction and hopped off and dashed across the street, through all the traffic and against all the safety rules I had ever heard. I got on the other bus and collapsed on a seat near the driver. I didn't see the green car. I took a deep breath — the first one in about five minutes, I figured — and kept my head turning, watching, watching for my stop near the bear pits, watching for the green car. When I didn't see the car for half a dozen blocks I felt a little better and when I got off the bus and looked up and down all the streets in sight and still didn't see it I felt better yet. But not for long.

I had walked half a block, perhaps, when around a corner came the car! The street they had turned into and the sidewalk that I was on edged a narrow park that sloped down to the river. At the end of the park were the bear pits and the bridge back to the center of town. Down near the river was a footpath to another, lower bridge that also led back to the center of town. There were trees and grass in the park but no shelter that would hide me from the street. The men in the green car would be able to see me no matter in which direction I went. But that fact — the fact that they couldn't help seeing me — gave me, suddenly, a plan.

I left the sidewalk and hurried toward the bear pits but instead of going to Ta'ab who was in the one spot out of view from the street I went straight into the ladies' room. The doorway to the ladies' room could be seen from the street except where it was blocked by the waist-high railing of the front pits so I came out on my hands and knees and crawled toward the back where I had left Ta'ab. I know I looked like an escaped idiot but I was so intent on what I was doing that I didn't think about that until much later. I found the Sultan and spoke quickly.

"Sulafa followed me and we must hurry! Count to a hundred and then go out to the street and back the way we came. Stay under those arches until you come to the big department store at the end. Go downstairs to the snack shop and wait for me. I think I can lose Sulafa."

Ta'ab only nodded and began to count. I crawled back to the ladies' room, stood up and went back out into the park — almost to the sidewalk. I bent down and pretended to tie my shoe, looking around for the green car. I saw it about half a block away and walked slowly until I thought they had seen me. Then I cut down through the park to the under bridge. It would take them quite a long time to go by road to that under level, I thought, and by that time I would be back at the department store. And that was the way it worked out. I found Ta'ab in the snack shop, we went together up and out of the store and onto the first bus out of town that we saw. To this day I remember it was headed for a place called Belp.

I have been boasting about how smart I was — and my plan did work very neatly — but now I have to confess that the rest of the day I was thoroughly shameful.

First of all as soon as I got on the bus and sat down I began to shake. My teeth chattered and I shivered all over and I would have burst into tears except that I *never* cry in public places. I was so close to breaking my rule that I could hardly focus on anything out of the bus window. It was just a blur of green fields and neat farmhouses with flowers in window boxes and it looked dreamlike and nice and that made me stop shivering.

Then I began to get angry. I was so mad at those stupid Arabs and that disgusting selfish Sultan and the more I thought about it the madder I got. I didn't want to be on a bus going to Belp! I didn't want to be hunted and chased! I didn't want to be wandering around where nobody knew where I was! And I didn't care what happened to Ta'abata Qabit or Shansharra or Jarjani or any of them! I didn't care if they all beheaded each other! I was *exploding* with anger. And right about then the bus began to slow down and a woman with two children began to move toward the door. I looked out the windows on both sides and all I saw was those peaceful green fields and without a word to Ta'ab I pushed across him and followed the woman and children to the door and out. I took the road that led away from the bus route and I walked as fast as I could, as if I had some important place to go. I didn't look around to see if Ta'ab had come too but I must have heard him drop from the bus for I knew he was behind me.

I walked on feeling scared, angry, sad, miserable, and not wanting to talk to anyone, especially Ta'ab, and for a long time he followed some distance behind me, not saying anything either. I didn't think of it at the time, being too busy feeling *my* feelings, but I suppose he was feeling scared, angry, sad and miserable too. He was even less used to thinking for himself than I was. We might have walked all the way to the end of that country road in silence except that we came to something that

107

felt even more scared and miserable than we did.

You have probably never seen an hérisson. I never had until I was in Switzerland. It has an English name but I forget what it is; I just learned about them as hérissons. They are little animals that look something like porcupines except they are much smaller — about the size of a kitten. They are prickly enough to keep dogs from eating them but they are harmless and round and cute. Drawings of them are used to decorate towels and boxes and cards and that sort of thing; if Walt Disney had been Swiss, Mickey Mouse would probably have been Henry Hérisson. Because they are so round and fat and short-legged they are very slow and they get run over on country roads quite often. That was what had happened here on the road we were walking. A mother hérisson had been hit by a car and was dead — which was sad and matched my gloomy mood perfectly — but near her and squealing in the most heartbroken way was her baby. He was a little round ball that just fit in my hand, so young that his spiny hair was still soft. I held him under my chin and smoothed his fur and tried to tell him not to cry — and for a little while he stopped.

By then Ta'ab was up with me. He inspected the mother, then the baby I was holding.

"Is it too young to leave its mother? Shall I kill it quickly?"

"No!" I shrieked. "How can all you people be so cruel!"

His answer was very mild.

"It is not cruel to prevent suffering!"

"It is if you could prevent suffering some other way! I could probably raise this baby! At least I could if I didn't have *you!*" It was a mean thing to say and he behaved a lot better than I would have. He took a step backward, there in the middle of the road and looked at me solemnly.

"I did not expect that you would have to be mixed up with our Samirian affairs so long as this. I am really sorry. Would you rather I left you alone and you could go back to your embassy without me?"

I stood there staring down at the baby hérisson in my hands and to my horror a tear plopped right on that baby's head. I turned away from Ta'ab and made myself stop crying while I thought about it. I really considered saying, Yes, go and leave me alone. But only for a minute. Then I turned around again and shook my head.

"No. I just want to sit down somewhere quiet and think for a while. And it will be better if we both use our heads." I forced a sort of weak smile and added, "We have a proverb that says, 'Two heads are better than one.' "

We walked along and I talked to the baby hérisson. It was probably terrified but I told myself it was comforted. When we came to a flat grassy spot we sat down and talked about our situation.

We could go back to the American Embassy but even if we had had an idea of how to get in without being seen it was too late in the afternoon to get there before it closed.

We could go back to the woods of Marcel Perriard—Maruqqish would still be there—but that did not seem to be a very good idea. I mean we would have been right back where we started.

"Shansharra has had two days," said Ta'ab. "Unless something has happened to him he must have many people looking for me. I wonder if we could telephone the hotel in Paris. I wonder if any of our people are still there."

"We could try to call," I suggested.

"How soon will someone begin looking for you?"

"Not until my parents get to Paris — four more days, I think. Unless someone discovers the things I left in the chair," I said, suddenly remembering. "Much good *that* did me!"

"What things? What chair?"

I told him about the letter and the postcard that I

110

had hidden in the chair and he looked at me in the funniest way and wanted to know who wrote them, where they came from, all about them and when he heard about Gordon Danko he jumped up, really excited.

"You mean you have a friend with a house somewhere here?"

"I guess so. Maybe. Unless he changed his plans. But I don't even remember the town or anything about it."

"But you have to! You have to! That is a place we could go and no one would look for us there. He can find Shansharra!"

"But I don't remember. He and his wife were going to stay at the house of some friend and they were going to stop at the school and see me but they didn't. That is absolutely all I remember."

"Everything you read makes an impression on your brain, you know. I will show you how to remember. But I have been thinking of something else. Have you noticed that not one car or person has come along this road? I think it would be good if we could stay out of sight in a place like this for a whole day. Or maybe two. Then if Sulafa and whoever was with him didn't see us on the streets or in any of the likely places they would think we had got clear away."

"Yes. That's a good — "

The baby hérisson began to cry again and I looked for something to feed him. I tried a blade of grass and a leaf of some sort. He did not want either of those. I felt around in my pockets and found a crumb left from the things we had eaten in Berne and he ate it right off my finger! He was a cooky eater!

"Look, Ta'ab. He does know how to eat!" I fished for more crumbs.

"Here's something better," said Ta'ab. "I still have a cooky left from the bear pit." He broke off tiny crumbs and we gave the baby as many as he would eat. Then he curled up in my lap and went to sleep.

"Let's call him Cooky," I suggested. Then I added, "I feel better now that he feels better."

Ta'ab nodded. He seemed to start to say something several times and finally did say, "That was a clever plan to get us away from the bear pits. How did you think of it?"

"I don't know. It just came to me."

"We have a proverb — "

"I'm sure!"

" 'Fear teaches how to run.' I guess that was it." I agreed. It probably was.

"Come on, Sarina. Let's walk as far as we can

before it gets dark. Perhaps we will see a place to spend the night."

I was fascinated with the sleeping Cooky on my lap but I slowly got up and followed and we did find a place, a perfect place, to spend the night.

Swiss farmhouses and their barns are usually in the same building but with their doors at opposite ends. This is important because when people — Ta'ab and I, for example — want to go into barns unseen, it makes it easier. Not only that, nearly all the barns have a road built up to their second floor. It is just a mound of dirt, really, that makes a narrow hill — wide enough for a truck or a wagon — leading up to the door in the top of the barn. It is for putting hay in, I think. Well, we found a barn like that.

All we had to do, we decided, was to go down the road a little distance, find another spot by the side to sit down and wait for it to get dark. It would be nice to say that while we were walking around waiting for it to be dark that we came on a place to buy some dinner, but we didn't. It was going to be another meal missed.

By now two or three cars had passed us and a string of children came by — from school, clearly, since they carried book bags. They all looked at us, one or two said Hi, but they didn't stop. The only people we talked to were three children who came by at dusk. They pulled a small cart.

They stopped and looked us over. One of them said something in German but when we answered in French the conversation switched over.

"Are you new here?"

"Visiting," I said.

"What are you doing with those cans?" asked Ta'ab, meaning the tall shiny cans in the cart.

"Taking milk to the dairy," said one of the children, a girl, in a puzzled voice, as if, How could anyone not know about taking the milk every evening?

"Would your baby animal drink milk?" Ta'ab asked me.

I showed them the baby hérisson in my lap and they came close to see it better.

"Could we try?" I asked. "Can you open the cans?"

"We are not supposed to take the tops off," said the tallest of the children, a boy. "But there is some milk spilled around the top. You could dip your finger in it."

I tried my finger but the space was too narrow. Then someone thought of a blade of grass and dipped it in, bringing up a tiny drop of milk. We splashed that one on the baby's nose and it ran off. And so did the second but a taste must have got into his mouth because he began to open it and look around for more. Everyone got blades of grass and we kept those drops coming until there was no more around the tops of the cans. The baby would have eaten more but at least we now knew two things we could feed it.

"We'd better go," said one of the children. "We'll see you later, maybe."

It was almost dark now and since we didn't want to see them later we waited until they were out of sight, watched to see that no cars were coming and then cautiously went to Our Barn. Maybe we were lucky or maybe it was easy but either way we walked up the drive to the top of the barn without being seen by farmer or farmer's dog or passerby or anybody.

Inside was an enormous room half filled with hay. Along one side the wall was hung with ropes and halters and bridles and things and in one corner were sacks full of grain or meal.

All my life I had wanted to spend a night in a barn. It was part of my wanting to be a heroine; I would have loved to be Heidi. You know, in that attic with the goats and the hay? So now I had visions of myself, cosily curled up in the sweet-smelling hay, lulled to sleep by the soft lowing of the cows in the bottom of the barn. Well, to begin with, through the cracks in the floor I could see that there were no cows in that barn. There was a horse, though, and telling myself I should be grateful for that, I set about making myself comfortable in the sweet-smelling hay. It did smell sweet, that much I can say, but that hay was the scratchiest, prickliest, most uncomfortable thing I ever tried to sit in. I'll take wet sand any day! So I finally went to the corner where the grain sacks were and the hay wasn't and I still felt itchy.

I tried to find a hollow space in one of the sacks or a snug place between them where the baby Cooky could spend the night but nothing seemed safe enough or warm enough. Ta'ab must have been watching for he suddenly leaned over me with his shoe in his hand.

"Here. Wouldn't he fit in this?"

He would and he seemed to like it. The shoe was warm, you see, and perhaps that was why he settled down and went to sleep. Ta'ab took shoe and Cooky and put them in a sheltered spot behind a grain bag.

"Now," said Ta'ab. "You must remember every word on that postcard."

"I can't!"

116

"Try! Start by thinking about the address. Make a picture of it in your mind."

I did that. It was clear enough. I told him how it had been addressed.

"How did he begin? Did he put a date? Did he sign his full name at the end or just one of his names?"

I knew that too. He had written "Gordon" with a "g" that was just a large version of a small "g."

"Now keep thinking of his writing. What else did he say? Where were the words on the postcard?"

"He began with something about roaming around Europe."

"Good. What did he end with?"

"He said they'd stop by the school — "

"The exact words!"

I closed my eyes tight.

" 'We will stop by the school to see you on our way.' I think that was it."

"Now," persisted Ta'ab, "go back and look at the whole thing in your mind. Make a picture of the beginning and the end and keep looking at it in your mind."

"I don't think — "

"Sh! Just do it! Even remember how the post-card felt in your hands."

So I looked and I looked in my mind and like

117

magic it gradually came. It was like those coloring books you paint over with water — things get clearer and clearer. I just whispered the words for fear they would disappear again.

"Village of Maxewil. Villa Raphael."

Ta'ab let out a deep breath.

"Good for you! Now let's go to sleep."

We pushed and pulled at those fat bags until we each got wedged in and could put our heads down. It had not been what I'd call the most restful day in my life but at least it made a sackful of meal seem like a downy pillow and I went to sleep at once. I was not nearly ready to wake up, either, when I heard the most hair-prickling sound you can imagine — something between a groan and a bellow.

X

*"Throw a lucky man into a river
and he will come up with a fish in his mouth."*

I SAT STRAIGHT UP — I would not be surprised if my hair were straight up too — to see Ta'ab crawling across the floor peering through the cracks.

"What is it?" I asked. "What is that absolutely curdling noise?"

"Sh! I'm trying to see if anyone is down there. The horse has colic."

"Colic?"

He didn't answer and kept crawling from crack to crack. Over one crack he paused a long time, moving his head back and forth to see better.

"That horse is going to have a foal!"

"Now? Is that why she has colic?"

"No, no! Colic is a stomach ache. But she will hurt herself and the baby if someone doesn't watch her. I'd better go down."

119

He stood up and went to the wall where the reins and ropes were hanging.

"You can't just go down and do something to someone else's horse! And it might not be what you say anyway!"

"You think I don't know when a horse has colic? I'm going down and walk her. That is the only thing to do. Otherwise she'll throw herself down and roll to try to get rid of the pain." He selected a halter from the wall.

I sighed.

"Do you want your other shoe?"

He hesitated, then shook his head, and, one shoe on, one shoe off, went out of the top of the barn and down the slope to the main barn door. I stood by the side of our upper door and watched.

For a while — nothing. Then there was another of those awful groan-bellows followed by a crash as if the horse were kicking at the wall or bumping it hard. Then silence. I began to worry about Ta'ab and started downward myself. I had almost reached the lower door when I saw moving shadows and heard the murmur of Ta'ab's voice. I backed up to let him lead the horse past.

"I'll just walk her until the pain is gone," he whispered.

I climbed back to our doorway and sat down to

wait since it didn't seem fair for me to go back to sleep. It was a clear night and there was a moon so I could watch Ta'ab's route. He went out to the main road and turned away from the house and barn and walked out of my sight, then a few minutes later he reappeared. He had almost reached the wagon track that led to the barn when a light bounced around the far corner of the house and headed toward the barn. A hand-held flashlight or lantern came closer and closer, directly to the barn door, and soon I was able to see two figures, a man and a boy.

The man switched on a light in the barn and saw at once that it was empty. They were pretty calm, I thought, considering that it looked as if their horse had just been rustled. On second thought, though, I was thinking like a girl who has seen about a million Western movies; Switzerland does not have horse rustlers. Which is why they got a lot more excited when they looked around and saw Ta'ab walking by with their horse!

They started calling out and running toward the street. I couldn't understand what they were saying — it was in German — but they sounded angry. I hesitated a moment, then followed them. I thought it would be easier for poor Ta'ab if he had me on his side to even the numbers. Poor Ta'ab! Ha. I should have known. I got there just in time for the meeting and Ta'ab was the first to speak.

"Someone let this mare eat too much green grass! She has colic." He said it more accusingly than explainingly and he said it in French. The boy understood and repeated it to the man, his father as it turned out.

Then they saw me. The father asked me several sharp questions but when I obviously did not understand, the boy translated.

Who were we? What were we doing? Why were we here? That sort of thing.

We answered with the barest explanations. I said we had sort of lost our way. Ta'ab said we were on our way to Maxewil. I hadn't thought of it that way since we didn't have any idea where Maxewil was but I guess we were at that.

The boy and his father discussed us for a while and the father seemed to be giving instructions. The boy explained.

"You" — he nodded at me — "will go with my father. There is.room in the house for you to sleep. I will stay and help to walk the horse. Then your brother will sleep in my room."

Ta'ab and I glanced at each other but we didn't say anything. It didn't matter. I started back toward the barn to get Cooky but the father took my arm and pulled me gently the other way. I couldn't explain to him about the baby hérisson so I called over my shoulder to Ta'ab, "Will you take care of Cooky?"

He agreed and I went with the farmer into the house.

He pointed to a chair and seemed to want me to sit down. Then he opened a door and I heard him say something beginning, "Mama — "

There was the sound of voices speaking softly and some moving around in that next room, then the man came out again with a woman. She had a sweet, fair face and a sympathetic smile and she began immediately to murmur and cluck over me — just like Mère Benedicte. She kept asking me things but I could only smile back at her. One of the things she asked must have been Was I hungry? because she went out of the room and came back with a glass of milk. I was really too sleepy to be hungry but I drank it. Then she took me by the hand and led me upstairs and into a tiny room under the roof. There was just room for a bed and a chest and it had a sloping ceiling with a window cut through it. It was so close to my Heidi dream that if I hadn't been so sleepy I would have giggled.

I took off my coat and sat down to take off my shoes and that would have been that — I was beginning to feel sewed into my clothes — but the woman disappeared and came back with a woolly nightgown. Then she patted me on the shoulder and left me alone.

I have told you about the best breakfast of my life. Well, this was the most welcome and wonderful bed.

Late the next morning Ta'ab and I had breakfast together while the woman hovered over us and kept bringing us more things to eat. Since we couldn't speak we smiled a lot. Ta'ab had found out quite a bit about the family while he and the boy had walked the horse. The parents were Papa and Mama Marbach. The boy, Tomas, was fourteen and there was a younger sister, Beatrice. It was Beatrice who had taken the horse out to feed on fresh grass and let it eat too much. Tomas and Beatrice were at school even though it was Saturday but they would be home about noon. Ta'ab and Tomas had fed Cooky more milk and crumbs and had found a box for him. The horse was Eva and she had recovered. All these things Ta'ab told me over breakfast.

"They don't seem very surprised to see us, do they?" I said.

"No," agreed Ta'ab. "That is odd, isn't it? Maybe we'll find out why when Tomas and his sister come home."

"Do they want us to stay here that long?"

Ta'ab nodded. "Tomas woke me up before he left to say he'd see me when he got back."

After breakfast we went to the barn to look at Cooky. As soon as he heard us he began to squeal and by the sound of his voice he was a lot stronger than he had been yesterday. Milk and bear cookies seemed to agree with him! Someone had left a jar of milk and a doll's bottle beside his box. I fed him from the tiny bottle while Ta'ab went to the horse's stall to see Eva. She was munching contentedly and looked so calm it was hard to believe she could either groan or bellow.

We were still in the barn when Tomas and his sister came home. This was my first real look at Tomas. He was tall and sturdy and had a thick fall of yellow hair across his forehead. Beatrice was eight years old, very solemn and very pretty; she spoke a little of both French and English. I'm sure it was because of Cooky but she became my devoted follower. She did not talk much but she never left my side unless she had to and she hardly took her eyes from my face. It made me uncom-

fortable at first — but I got used to it very soon. Liked it even. The last few days had not been overfilled with admiring looks!

I thought that as soon as Tomas came home and could act as translator that the parents would ask us questions. They did — but not the ones I had expected. Not who were we, where were our parents, where did we come from. Instead the first was, "Why are you going to Maxewil?"

"We think we have a friend there," I answered.

When the mother heard that answer she shook her head and even I could understand the Nein and No gut. She ended, Tomas translated, by saying that the Red Cross was better.

We were puzzled but had enough sense not to say anything just then.

The other question was to Ta'ab and I found it as odd as the first one.

Did he play futbol? Ta'ab said he did.

After lunch the children had chores to do. Beatrice had to weed the vegetable garden. Since she was so worshipful the least I could do was to help her, I thought, but Tomas said, firmly, "No. Beatrice will work faster alone. It is better if you come with me." Then he added something to Beatrice and she smiled and nodded and ran off to begin. Tomas explained to us, "We have a field of potatoes not far from here. It has been turned this morning and I am to take a wagon and collect the potatoes. If you will help it will not take long. I told Beatrice that when she finishes she can join us and we will all ride home together."

It did not occur to him that we might not want to help pick up potatoes — but of course we did want to help. Even Ta'ab seemed to think it perfectly reasonable, though it must surely be the first time he had ever been invited to do farmwork!

Tomas and Ta'ab hitched Eva to the wagon and we all climbed aboard. As soon as we were settled I asked about those words that had been bouncing around in my head ever since I had heard them. The Red Cross.

"What was it your mother said about the Red Cross?" I asked.

"They take care of all the refugees. It is better that you go to them. If there are friends in Maxewil, the Red Cross will find them for you."

There was a pause and then I said, carefully and, I hoped, casually, "Do you have many refugees here?"

"Not dozens, you understand, but every little while there are one or two. Especially in summer when it is easy to get over the mountain passes."

It did not seem strange to him and he, like his parents, seemed certain that we were two more refugees. I don't know about Ta'ab but I just barely knew what a refugee was. Something like a fugitive, someone who was running away, I thought. But I had no idea where the refugees he was talking about were running from. It made it a very dangerous subject.

"Has your mother called the Red Cross?" asked Ta'ab, as carefully as I had asked my question.

"Oh, no. The Red Cross office is not open on Saturdays. She will take you on Monday. Besides, she likes to have them—you—uh, the refugees—" (it seemed to make him uncomfortable to talk about it) "stay over for a day or two. She says a day of good food and good rest helps make up for the past."

I nodded and Ta'ab changed the subject to futbol.

Tomas loved futbol! (They call it that but I think it is really soccer.) Tomas told us all about his team and the opposing team and about the best players and about the game that evening. He said that Ta'ab would be welcomed as a player in that game because one of the regulars couldn't play. And one of the reasons Tomas was so eager to finish the potatoes was so he would have time to practice with

Ta'ab before dinner. I really didn't listen to it all — I don't know anything about that game except that it is called football but isn't. Not our football, anyway.

That conversation lasted all the way to the field and through most of the potato gathering. I preferred picking up potatoes. It was a very large field, though, and that is a lot of bending over and standing up. We were nearly finished when Beatrice came and I was very glad to see my little shadow.

When we left for the farm there was an enormous pile of potatoes in the wagon — more potatoes than I had ever seen in one place.

"Do you sell these," asked Ta'ab, "or do you keep them for yourselves?"

He was still getting the international viewpoint, I supposed. Tomas said, "Both. We keep enough for our family in the cellar and sell the rest."

Beatrice had been watching my face. When there was a pause she said, "You don't look sad. Are you?"

I shook my head.

"Mother said I shouldn't talk to you — about — you know — where you came from — because it is too painful — "

"Then why are you?" asked her brother.

130

She was silent and Ta'ab changed the subject. Again. And in my head I was saying, Good boy!

"Can Sarina and Beatrice come to the futbol game too?" he asked.

And that got us on safe ground. And, Yes, the girls were permitted to come to the game. And we did.

Papa Marbach and the four of us, after an early dinner, walked to the futbol field. It wasn't a stadium or anything grand — just a field with goal posts and a double row of benches along each side. I watched that game hard from beginning to end and I still don't know anything about soccer. The best part is when players hit the ball with their heads — I saw Ta'ab do that several times. I could not tell whether Ta'ab was a good player or not but he seemed to be a fast runner. By the end of the first few minutes his face was red and shiny and he looked like any other of those Swiss boys. He yelled and kicked and bumped the ball and banged into other players just like the rest of them. I hate to tell you this but Beatrice had to tell me who won!

On the way home there were a few minutes when Ta'ab and I were alone. I said, "You played very well. Did you enjoy it?"

He was still a little breathless.

131

"Best game I was ever in! Did you see the boy named Hermann? What a kicker!"

He looked back at some of the boys who were walking behind us.

"It must be a fine thing to be a boy like that. Not to have to worry about being a ruler and the international viewpoint and all that."

"It is much harder for you," I agreed. "You'll have to make up for it by being a really terrific sultan."

"I will be," he said. "Maybe the boys of Samir — and the girls too — will be able to — "

His voice trailed off and he was staring past me as if he were looking into time or space. I think maybe he was. I think maybe that was the beginning.

Then we were included in the group and went the rest of the way home.

Later Beatrice and Tomas and Ta'ab and I all went to the barn. Mama Marbach had given us some crisp crackers and Cooky liked those crumbs too. He seemed so happy in his box and with his new life that I had stopped worrying about him. He was going to survive.

While Beatrice was feeding Cooky and Tomas

was holding a pail of oats for Eva I talked to Ta'ab alone again for a moment.

"How are we going to get away? Can we stay through tomorrow? Or should we leave tonight?"

"What about telling Tomas who we really are?" suggested Ta'ab, without really answering my questions.

I looked at Tomas. Would he believe us? Could he be trusted?

"Yes. Let's do," I said.

"Good. I think so too. When it is quiet tonight, come down to his room. I'll explain we have something to tell him."

I nodded and went back to help Beatrice.

The house was quiet. Ta'ab, Tomas and I sat on the floor, whispering. Ta'ab had not told Tomas anything except that we had something we had to explain to him. Which was very thoughtful, considering that he could have blurted the whole thing out and had all the surprise to himself. As it was, Ta'ab began by getting a promise.

"We are going to tell you something you will find hard to believe but you must believe us enough not to repeat it to anybody at all."

"That's right," I joined in. "But just for a few

days. And when you *can* tell it you will have a wonderful story."

Tomas looked doubtful for about three seconds and then I guess he decided we couldn't be escaped bank robbers.

"Not anybody?"

Ta'ab and I shook our heads solemnly.

"Not until we give you permission."

"Agreed, then."

Ta'ab and I looked at each other. Where to begin?

"For one thing," I said, "we are not related."

"And we are not refugees," added Ta'ab.

"I am Sarina Thorpe and I am an American. This is His Royal Highness, the Sultan of Samir. Ta'abata Qabit."

Tomas pushed that hanging blond lock off his forehead and I think he was about to argue with us, to tell us that that was impossible, but Ta'ab took up the story.

"It's true. If you get me an atlas I will show you Samir. If you give me pencil and paper I will write for you in Arabic. And Sarina's parents are archeologists; they live in California. It is all true."

I had a funny thought that two days ago Ta'ab would not have understood how odd a story ours was; he would not have explained and offered

134

proof. He would have pulled himself to full height and said, 'Do you dare doubt the word of a sultan? Hurrumph, hurrumph!' I was really beginning to like this new Ta'abata Qabit. Now he was saying, "But what happened to get us here is even more complicated and astonishing."

To look at Tomas you would not think anything could be more astonishing than what he had already heard. He kept murmuring, "A sultan! California!" and pushing back that hair until by the end of our story he looked like a blond rooster!

At one point I interrupted to ask, "Tomas, has there been anything about us in the newspaper? Or on the radio?"

"Not that I know about, not that I have heard. But then where did you go — after the night in the woods?"

We finished the story and Ta'ab concluded, "We haven't decided for sure but I think we should leave early tomorrow morning before your family is awake. You can explain to them that it was necessary and that in a few days we will explain everything."

"And you could say that we thank them and have enjoyed being here," I added.

"Yes, yes. Of course," said Tomas. "But wait. You must get to Maxewil, you say."

"Where is that, exactly?" I asked.

"You don't know where Maxewil is?" That was the only time when I think he doubted our story for a moment. "But it is not far from here. You did not know that?"

We shook our heads.

"But you said you were on your way there!"

Well, yes, but — We explained again.

He shook his head in wonderment and that topknot waved back and forth.

"Incredible! Because if you had set out from Geneva to go to Maxewil you could not have gone more directly. It is a little more than forty kilometers from here, near Interlaken. What luck you have had!"

" 'Throw a lucky man into a river and he will come up with a fish in his mouth!' " said Ta'ab, laughing.

"That's a proverb," I explained. "He knows millions of them. But we have been lucky. You and your family have been our lucky fish!"

"Then," Ta'ab asked, "if we started walking early in the morning we could get there by tomorrow afternoon?"

"Of course. Also there are two bus routes from here. Plus the train."

"Not the train. They are too easy to watch."

136

"It would be best to get there without using the roads at all, would it not?" asked Tomas.

We stared at him. How do you get someplace without using the roads?

Without waiting for us to ask the question he went on, faster and faster, more and more excited, with the most marvelous plan to get us to Maxewil.

And we did not use the roads. Well, hardly.

XI

*"If thou canst not take a thing by the head,
then take it by the tail."*

NEARLY EVERY Sunday afternoon, we were told, when the weather was pleasant the Marbach family drove to a nearby airfield. A cousin, Rudolf, was pilot of a small airplane that towed gliders to a position where they could cut themselves loose and float back down to the field. He often took the children up on one of his short flights. What made it so perfect for Tomas' plan and for us was that his glider-towing took him back and forth between this field and an Interlaken field. We talked about gliding on the drive out to the field. Ta'ab was full of questions. He wanted to know all about gliders, what they were useful for (they are not very useful — mostly for sport), how big a plane was needed to pull them, things like that. More international viewpoint.

Before we arrived Tomas began his plan for us.

"It would be exciting," he said, "for Ta'ab and Sarina if they could fly with Cousin Rudolf. May I ask him?"

Papa Marbach said, and Tomas translated with a grin, "You may ask him — but don't argue!"

I could not see how Tomas was going to persuade his cousin without telling him our story but he seemed sure that he knew what he was doing.

Apparently he did too. He went alone to the hangar to help Rudolf get the plane ready. They both came back to the car. Rudolf was a tall young man with spiky black hair and a small mustache. He had a scarf around his neck and looked like an aviator in an old movie. In fact, he looked like the Red Baron.

When we were introduced he said, "Tomas tells me you'd like to try my wings." He asked something of the Marbachs, their consent, apparently, and they nodded. It was arranged as easily as that.

The hard thing was to say goodby to the Marbachs as if I'd be back in twenty minutes. Especially to Beatrice. On the walk to the plane I said to Tomas, "Will you give Cooky to Beatrice for me? And tell her I wish she were my little sister? And tell your parents — "

"Yes, yes. I'll take care of it all."

139

"And," said Ta'ab, "we'll let you know how it turns out as soon as we can."

When we were settled and ready to leave, Tomas wished us luck and repeated to Rudolf, "Don't forget to put them on the right road for Maxewil!" and we were off.

The plane skimmed just over treetops it seemed — not like big passenger planes, the only kind I had been on. I could see everything that was happening below — children playing, horses running, people waving — I loved it! It did not last long enough though. We were landing again in about fifteen minutes at a field that looked just like the one we had left.

"This is the Interlaken field," said Rudolf, "but of course it is far from town. Come with me and I'll show you how to go."

For a time we would follow another of those public foot trails and he took us to the beginning of that. We were to watch for a road that crossed it soon. We were to turn toward the mountains on that road, he said, and it would lead us to the village of Maxewil. That last stretch would be the only time we were on public road.

We tried to thank him but he would not listen.

"I have never had a mystery in my life before. That's why I fly — life is not exciting enough. So just let me hear the whole story someday and that will be thanks and more."

Tomas had known his cousin well.

The directions were easy to follow and we soon came to the road to Maxewil. It curved steeply along the edge of a mountain valley. From the grassy edge of the road we looked over some scary drops straight down. The road rounded a final curve and there was Maxewil. Buildings lined the central square, scattered houses stood on the hillsides. The road went past and on up the mountain.

It was late afternoon. There were people sitting in the square and in the cafés but the stores were closed. Even the kiosks were closed. We stood at the edge of the square, uncertain. Where could we ask directions? Then we saw a woman come into the square carrying a basket of groceries. We both had the same idea — a market owner would know the local houses — and we hurried the way she had come. Sure enough, there was a tiny market — more of a milk store, I guess — open.

My advice to you is to learn how to say "Where is — " in every language in the world. It would have been very useful that afternoon. As it was, we stood in that little store and said "Villa Raphael" over and over to a very puzzled woman. She

141

seemed to think we had come to pick up an order of groceries and kept looking through a set of papers trying to find it. We pointed out the door and she nodded and kept looking for an order. Finally, I took a pencil from a jar near the cash register and a sack that lay nearby and drew an X and pointed to the floor, meaning that stood for where we were. She nodded. Then I drew a line that was meant to be the street and I pointed and again she nodded. Then at the end of that line I drew another X and wrote Villa Raphael beside it. A brilliant smile. At last she knew what we wanted! She took the pencil, erased my Villa Raphael, drew another street and made another X. Then she took us to the door and pointed. We thanked her, took our precious map-sack and left.

The road she had pointed to led from one side of the public square to a cluster of houses on the hillside. It was narrow, steep and winding. We had barely started the climb when a car came toward us — a green car. I grabbed Ta'ab and we flattened ourselves against a wall. It was not even the same color of green as the one Sulafa had been driving but I had a sudden hatred of all green cars. This one had two men in it and they looked hard at us as they went down the hill.

Around the next bend was an iron gate and

the sign on one of the posts said, Villa Raphael!

"Now, may your friend still be here. *Insha'allah.*"

Ta'ab was figuring out how the gate opened when that same car came back again very slowly. One of the men leaned out and said to Ta'ab, "Your Highness?"

Ta'ab just stared. I think he was trying to decide whether to admit it or not. He had not moved when the man went on, "It is quite all right. We are police. Go up to the house; you will be welcome there."

Now those sound like warm and friendly words, don't they? But we were so suspicious that we were not sure. Welcomed by what people? Had Jarjani's men outwitted us? Were they inside the house? Of course *they* would welcome us!

We walked cautiously up the path toward the house. It was a big wooden house with at least three stories to it and each floor had its own balcony. As we came in sight of the main door we heard a shout and some loud voices.

To show you how we had reached the point where we expected bad surprises much sooner than good surprises, when we heard that shout Ta'ab and I without one word to each other dove off the pathway and behind a bush. There was silence; a long silence. Then there seemed to be footsteps on the walk — as cautious as ours had been. We peeked through the branches and there, looking around in a puzzled way, was my father!

I don't even remember what happened next. We were surrounded, I know that. And hugged and patted and examined and hugged again. And introduced.

By that time the two men we had met in the road had come into the house, too, and that made a large crowd. My mother and father. Gordon and Betsy Danko. (I didn't get to know Betsy until later but I liked her the minute I looked at her. She has long, dark red hair and a friendly smile and a nice quiet way of saying funny things — but that day I just saw the hair and the smile.) Shansharra was there with two other loyal Samirians — and if I was being fussed over by my parents you should have seen those men with the Sultan! The two men who followed us in were agents from the International Police. Interpol, they call it. It is a network of police offices all through Europe and the world and they work together to catch criminals that go from one country to another. Lieutenant Comte was the Swiss representative and Lieutenant Hedard was from Paris. The only one missing was Maruqqish. Ta'ab and I explained where we had left him and asked if we could go for him right away. No one thought that would be a good idea but Lieutenant Comte said he would call the Geneva office. If they could spare a man they would bring him to us.

Naturally, the most important thing after they found out that Ta'ab and I had no broken bones or anything was to find out what happened. And we were pretty curious about what happened ourselves. So bit by bit we got the whole story. It came out all mixed up — a little part from the beginning, a little part from the end, with Ta'ab and me telling our side of it from time to time. I've put it in order.

On Thursday morning, the day I went into Ta'ab's room, Shansharra and the two other loyal Samirians had gone to make a diplomatic visit to someone in the French government. During the meeting Sulafa called to that office and told Shansharra that His Highness, the Sultan, had had a sudden stomach cramp and had been rushed to the hospital. He gave the Regent the name and address of a hospital that was quite distant from the hotel and in the opposite direction from the airport. By the time Shansharra discovered the mistake and rushed back to the hotel the Sultan and the plotters would have been on an airplane — except that Maruqqish spoiled their plan.

At the hospital Shansharra was worried and a little suspicious but until he reached the hotel he did not realize what an enormous crime was under way. Then the first call he made was to the airport. He was able to find out that a plane had been chartered for a flight to Samir. He rushed to the airport but of course no one came to take that waiting plane. From the airport he called Samir. No one back there among Shansharra's trusted staff knew anything about anything. Next Shansharra called back to the hotel. No one at the desk there knew of anything unusual — just that no one answered when they rang the Sultan's room.

Have you noticed how much of this whole adventure was arranged by telephone calls? Have you thought how people can call you and sound official and you will believe them? I mean, suppose Mrs. Bates is the principal's secretary and she calls from your school. You know who she is but you have never talked to her on the phone. Suppose this voice that says it is Mrs. Bates from the school tells you that there is a meeting of certain students, including you, an hour before school begins the next day. Wouldn't you believe it? And go to school early? Even if it didn't sound like her you would just say, She sounds different on the phone. You just wouldn't doubt it. Maybe it will be a good thing when they get those phones you can see through.

Well, anyway, there was Shansharra making calls from the airport. He was mystified, frightened for the Sultan's safety and furious that such a plot had been planned under his own unseeing eyes. He also was limited in men and one of the ablest, Maruq-qish, had disappeared too. There was another difficulty. He wanted the Sultan safe at all costs. At the same time he did not want anyone to know that the Sultan was missing. If you are a regent you can't go around misplacing sultans! So he was feeling quite helpless and desperate and it was already late in the afternoon when he took a taxi to the office of Interpol.

Lieutenant Hedard took up the story.

"When Monsieur Shansharra arrived we began at once to make the search. But first we had to find a picture of the Sultan and make copies of it."

He reached into a pocket and pulled out a photograph. It showed a round-faced, solemn boy with long hair in Arab robes — hardly anyone would have recognized Ta'abata Qabit from that! Ta'ab and I grinned at each other. Lieutenant Hedard continued.

"We checked hospitals, planes and trains. We made a routine search of the hotel room." He

148

smiled at me. "We found your letter and postcard almost immediately but we did not know what to make of them. When we inquired at the desk and they said you had been checked out by a nun we dropped the matter and continued with our other investigations.

"We got word late Thursday evening that His Highness had crossed the border into Switzerland. I brought my Swiss colleague, Lieutenant Comte, into the search and Monsieur Shansharra and I went to Geneva. The three of us met together early the next morning."

Lieutenant Comte was a tall man with a thin gray mustache and a thin straight mouth but his blue eyes had a little twinkle so that he seemed to be smiling even when his mouth wasn't.

"Later that same evening I spoke to the customs officer at the border. He remembered speaking with the Samirian Secretary; he had not seen the party, however. As part of diplomatic courtesy he agreed not to disturb His Highness." Lieutenant Comte turned to me.

"Do you see how it was? We still did not know about you!"

"When did you find out about what happened at the hotel in Geneva and about the fight between Jarjani and Maruqqish?"

"A policeman arrived to find three Arabs leaning over Jarjani. He had Jarjani taken to the prison hospital and kept the others overnight in jail while he checked their stories. They, of course, put all the blame on Maruqqish. They were all released in the morning. That was Friday."

"We were having strawberries and cream in the forest!" I said.

"Jarjani and his men were released before I knew I was looking for them," continued Lieutenant Comte, with a faint, slightly bitter smile. "The Trade Mission of Samir told us they knew absolutely nothing of the Sultan's whereabouts and were most eager to be kept informed of anything we found out."

"No doubt," grunted Shansharra.

"We traced Ta'abata to the hotel fairly soon that morning. There was no mystery about that — reservations had been made for the Sultan's party. When the elevator boy arrived for work we were waiting for him and he gave us a complete story of all that he had seen. He was the first to tell us that there was a girl in the group."

"What happened to the Second Secretary?" asked Ta'ab. "When we saw him last he was unconscious in a linen closet."

"No one at the hotel saw him again and we

haven't found him. We assume he regained con-
sciousness and let himself out."

"He might have been one of the men in the green
car — I couldn't tell," I said.

"Yes. He might have been. Well, there we were.
It was well into Friday morning. We had a missing
sultan. We had a missing man — Maruqqish —
possibly wounded. We had a missing — and
mysterious — girl who might be Sarina Thorpe.
After all, there was no way so far to connect that
mail in the Paris hotel with the girl in the Geneva
hotel.

"We set a man to checking with the nuns who
run the school. It took him most of that day but he
did discover that there had been no call from the
mother superior to the Paris hotel.

"Then we began trying to get word to the
Thorpes in Bulgaria and to the Dankos here. The
Dankos were easy. And helpful. Said we could use
the house here as clearing house for information.
We kept this phone open for incoming calls. But it
was past midnight when we got through to Professor Thorpe."

"Ooh! Were you pretty worried?" I asked.

"Worried!" My mother's voice went up in a little
screech. She didn't have to say anything more.

"We tried to leave that night but it was impossible," rumbled my father. "We had to settle for a flight early the next morning."

"They were rather calm, considering everything," said Gordon with a grin. "They only telephoned twice during the rest of that night!"

"Oh, I know!" my mother said apologetically. "We kept waking you up!"

"So then what happened?"

Lieutenant Hedard went on with the story.

"On Friday afternoon something very odd happened. One of the Samirian men was checking at railway stations in small towns in the area between Geneva and Berne. On one stop he had occasion to walk past a parked camper and from it came familiar music — folk songs from Samir. He got very excited, opened the door and looked in and saw a young man with a guitar on his knees, listening to a small tape recorder.

"Michael O'Duffy!" said Ta'ab and I.

Lieutenant Hedard nodded.

"He did not think the boy who taught him the songs could be the boy in our picture but he told the agent that he had taken you to the American Embassy. So that became our next point of investigation."

"When was this?" Ta'ab wanted to know.

"Midafternoon Friday."

"Were you there before I came back?" I asked.

"You didn't come back. We waited all afternoon."

"I did come back but — " I told about the men in the green car, waiting. About my turnabout on the buses. About my marvelous plan.

"She is very clever," interrupted Ta'ab at one point and I did not even try to look modest.

"But how did Jarjani know that we were going to come back to the embassy?" I wondered.

"The American Junior Secretary called the Trade Mission to check on your story and mentioned that you both would return later in the afternoon. Someone there must have been in touch with Jarjani. As for us, we were waiting inside and by the end of the afternoon when you had not arrived we gave up.

"All that night and all day Saturday we had men searching. It is hard to see how two sets of people could disappear so completely in such a small country!"

"I wish," said Lieutenant Hedard, "that people would mislay themselves any time except on weekends. Nearly everyone we wanted to talk to had gone out of town!"

"We had gone out of town too," said Ta'ab. "We had gone to Belp!"

"Ta'ab was helping the soccer team win its Saturday game," I added.

"We had men covering airports, charter plane companies, rail stations, all border crossings — and even with all that you found us before we found you," said Lieutenant Comte, shaking his head.

"But we have used some special methods," said Ta'ab.

"And stayed in some unusual places!" I added.

"Yes. We haven't men enough or time enough to stop at every farm and search through every small wood!"

Lieutenant Hedard had been looking thoughtfully at me. After a moment he spoke hesitantly. "I have been thinking how you, Mademoiselle Sarina, led the men in the green car away from the Sultan. I wonder if they would follow the decoy again."

"No!" said my mother.

"What were you thinking?" asked Ta'ab.

"I have thought that if we could bring the leaders as far as the road to Maxewil it would be an excellent place to capture them."

" 'If thou canst not take a thing by the head, then take it by the tail,' " said Ta'ab, grinning at me.

Lieutenant Comte was excited.

154

"Yes," he said. "We could bring them as far as Interlaken with a call to the Trade Mission. They obviously have an informer in that office."

"And Mademoiselle could —"

"No!" said my mother again.

"It would be perfectly safe," said Lieutenant Hedard. "We would have our men near her at all times."

"Then why could you not arrest the men in Interlaken?" asked my father.

"In a busy little town like that police are hampered by the innocent people who also fill the streets. And there is too much chance of their escaping."

"Then," persisted my father, "why couldn't you bring them straight to Maxewil with your phone call to the Trade Mission?"

Again the Interpol men had an answer.

"Because there are three roads leading into Maxewil. If we had enough men to control them all I fear we would be seen and Jarjani would not enter the trap."

"She will be quite safe," repeated Lieutenant Hedard.

"Don't forget that she is very clever," said the Sultan.

"We will arrange that she is never out of sight of

her father," suggested Lieutenant Comte. And with that it was decided that tomorrow morning I would go out by myself and be the lamb that led the wolves into the trap.

XII

"He that betrays one that betrays him not,
Allah shall betray him."

IT WAS like a party with so many people in that big house. My mother hovered over me at first, touching me every now and then, as if to see if I were real, but by the next morning she had got used to having me back. She even tried to be enthusiastic about my going out alone on my adventure that morning. I could tell she wasn't really happy about it, though, because she kept warning everyone. She did it in the half-laughing way she has but she was serious. She warned me about a million times to be careful. She warned my father not to let me out of his sight. She warned Lieutenant Hedard not to let my father out of *his* sight. She — well, you see how it was.

As for me, I could hardly wait! I was all ready to be a heroine again.

Lieutenant Comte called the Samirian Trade Mission right after breakfast. He was a good actor! His side of the conversation went like this:

"I have been told by the Swiss police that two children of the proper ages and description have been seen in Interlaken. Do you have any information that could confirm this?"

* * * * *

"No?"

* * * * *

"Well, no doubt it is a false report. You know how these things are."

* * * * *

"Yes, yes of course. I will get in touch with you again."

He turned from the phone.

"If they leave immediately it will take two hours to arrive — at the earliest."

Soon after that Lieutenant Comte received a phone call. He told us, frowning, "One of our men has spoken to Marcel Perriard. Your Maruqqish left him early yesterday morning. He should not have left so soon but he insisted."

It was as if something cold touched my back and from the blank look on Ta'ab's face I could tell he was worried too. It darkened the day a little.

When the time came my father and Lieutenant Comte and I got into Gordon's little yellow sports car. Lieutenant Comte showed us the spot on the square in Maxewil where one group of police would be stationed. It was at the top end of the twisty road from Interlaken. There would be another group at the bottom of the road. Jarjani's men would be trapped between the two.

They let me out in the middle of Interlaken. I was to walk around the main shopping streets that surrounded the center park. I could ask at various shops how to get to Maxewil if I wanted. I could look in shop windows too. I should be natural and try not to look as if I were looking for someone.

I did as I was told. I must have looked at a million watches. I must have had five sets of directions on how to get to Maxewil. I kept passing the same people on my trips around — a group of hikers in short leather pants taking pictures of each other with the *Jungfrau* in the background, two old ladies doing the same thing. I went around the park three times and the only thing that happened was that I found out a really good way to see what is going on without having anyone know you are looking. You watch reflections in the windows you are looking in. It got so I didn't even see the jewelry and stuff in the windows — I just saw what was going on behind my back. Somewhere in the background I could always see the yellow car, which was comforting, but I almost gave up seeing any Arabs. Perhaps they had not accepted the bait.

It was on the fourth time around the park that I saw the same green car I'd seen in Berne. Full of Arabs! For a minute I didn't like being where I was — exposed like that — and alone. But I took a deep breath, took a hopeful look at the yellow car and went on with my job.

It was about two blocks later that I felt certain I had been seen and was being followed. Without looking back I started for the Maxewil road. At the beginning of the climb I did not see anyone at all. I was not certain that the trick had worked until at one sharp curve I could look back along the road and see the green car and, some distance behind it, the yellow car. I continued. I climbed higher and higher until I had reached the section where the side of the road dropped off steeply. I was walking on the inside, next to the mountain, when I suddenly heard an odd sound — a muffled mixture of hoofs and bells — and before I could guess what it was a herd of cows came around a curve.

There were perhaps twenty of those furry brown Swiss cows that look like big mice and behind them a man and two boys. I flattened myself against the cliff to let them pass. Six or eight had gone by when the green car appeared on the road.

If the car had stopped quietly I think the cows would have gone around it and been past in a few minutes. Instead of waiting quietly, however, the driver began angrily to honk the horn. That startled the cows so that they all stopped right where they were except for the ones in front, closest to the loud horn, who turned around and started to go back up the hill. That made them all shuffle around nervously without really moving from where they stood.

This stretch of road had a curve at both ends. The cows were taking up most of it up to the upper end. The green car was at the lower end. That left the yellow car with my father in it around the lower curve and out of sight. My mother would have been furious! But I hardly gave that a thought because I suddenly saw two other things that took all my attention.

The first thing I noticed was that one of the two boys with the herd was Ta'abata! He was supposed to be back at the house but here he was.

The other thing I saw, now that the green car was just a few cows away from me, was that the man in the front seat beside the driver was Maruqqish.

I slid along the cliff, through and around the cows, until I could call to Ta'ab.

"It's Maruqqish! Can you see him?"

Ta'ab nodded and began working his way toward me. The driver was honking the car horn still and the man and the boy were yelling at the cows to try to move them forward. I think I could say it was pandemonium.

Then Ta'ab was almost beside me and said quickly, "See if you can get the herdsmen to keep the cows where they are — blocking the road just this way. I'm going down there."

"No!" I screamed, grabbing at him. "You can't!"

"If they keep the cows steady it will be all right," he said. "Don't you remember Ulysses?" He shook off my hand and moved forward through the herd of cows.

Ulysses? Oh, Ulysses! I did remember and it might work. I hurried to the boy and asked him not to move the cows, to keep them where they were. It was important, I said. A man's life depended on it!

I hardly waited for his answer because, scary as it was, I had to see what Ta'ab was going to do. We never saw those two Swiss farmers after that day and I didn't notice how they managed it but that herd of cows stood right there during the rest of the episode. I guess they were as important in this story as anyone else.

Ta'ab wove in and out through the cows until he was within shouting distance of the car. Then he stopped. I don't know how soon Jarjani and Zuhir and the rest recognized Ta'ab. By the time he started yelling at them in Arabic, surely. I couldn't tell exactly what he was saying, of course, but I could guess by what happened. After the first exchange the car door opened and Maruqqish stumbled out. His hands were tied behind his back; he looked white and ill. Behind him, through the car window, leaned Jarjani. There was a gun in his hand and it was pointed at Maruqqish's back. I thought he was going to shoot him but as Maruqqish started toward Ta'ab and nothing happened I could see that he was just threatening to shoot him. That was Jarjani's way of keeping him under control.

For a few seconds it seemed like one of those stop-action shots — Ta'ab and I and the cows and Jarjani with the gun — all motionless.

During that motionless moment Ta'ab, without looking at me, called my name.

"Sarina! Be ready!"

I thought I knew what he meant and I was ready.

163

Maruqqish moved toward Ta'ab slowly, unsteadily, the gun behind him pointed firmly. There was the slightest pause — like a catch of breath — when Ta'ab and Maruqqish looked at each other across the backs of two cows and then they both disappeared. That was my signal and I dropped to my hands and knees and started crawling for the curve at the upper end of that stretch of road. I crawled through the legs of those cows — it was a funny sight; like a forest of skinny legs — and caught up with Maruqqish who had to go very slowly because of his arms being tied. We went the rest of the way together but as we came to the last of the herd, still staying as low as we could, we heard behind us the racing motor of the car. With horn honking viciously, with a squealing of tires and a roaring of the engine it seemed as if they would drive right through both the herd of cows and us. But just after that there was another squeal of brakes and then a grinding, smashing, tearing, endless crash. I think it was the most horrible sound I have ever heard and it seemed to go on and on and on.

Maruqqish and I stood up and went to the edge of the road; Ta'ab, who had already gone around the curve to wait for us, came back; my father appeared from somewhere and put his arm around me. (He had walked up the road when the yellow car got stopped around the curve but I had not seen him.)

There below us was the green car on its side. One of the wheels was still spinning but otherwise there was no sign of movement. There was a white mound about halfway down but which man lay motionless under those robes I could not tell. We were all of us shocked and silent. Maruqqish and I sat down right where we were and I pulled my father with me. I didn't want to let go of his hand. Ta'abata Qabit stood a little longer, looking down. "He that betrays one that betrays him not, Allah shall betray him," he murmured. There was a faint look of satisfaction on his face and for once I really couldn't blame him.

And by that time we were surrounded by police and the Interpol men. It was all over.

None of us stayed in Maxewil very long after that. We all had our interrupted plans to go back to. It was sad, in a way, saying goodby to Ta'ab. We were going to such different worlds and perhaps would never see each other again. The last time we had a chance really to talk was shortly before he and Shansharra and Maruqqish left.

"Do you think Tomas would like a horse?" Ta'ab asked me.

I must have looked blank because he went on, "I would like to send him something. We raise excellent Arabian horses in Samir."

"Of course he would! That would be a wonderful thing to do."

"And what do you think for Monsieur Perriard?"

We thought for a moment.

"What about a greenhouse?" I suggested. "One of those glass rooms for growing things in. So he could grow enough to make up for the shrinking forest."

"Good idea. I'll have that done. I thought I would invite Cousin Rudolf to visit Samir. Remember how he wanted some excitement? Do you think he would find that exciting enough?"

I nodded. Then someone came in and that was the last time we talked together — except to say Goodby and Don't forget to write and that sort of thing.

We do send letters once in a while, Ta'ab and Tomas and I, and one day soon after we got home there was a package for me from Samir. It held a bracelet of gold and opals — the most beautiful and delicate thing I have ever seen. The card said,

167

"From three grateful Samirians" — and was signed by Ta'ab and Shansharra and Maruqqish.

The bad part about an adventure is that afterwards you know you'll probably never have another one like it. Or maybe none at all. In the last three years the most exciting thing that happened was a landslide that blocked our road. Someone told me, though, that there is a different kind of adventure — inner adventure — I think it was — and I am looking forward to discovering it.

Anyway, I'll never forget my week with Ta'ab. One odd little thing is that I seem to have developed an international viewpoint myself without even knowing it. I read the international news every day and the other morning I saw something in the paper that shows how important our week was for Ta'ab, too. It was a big article on the front page. SAMIR WINS INTERNATIONAL PEACE PRIZE. The prize was given because of many things the little country had done to encourage peace among its neighbors and to get them all to work together to improve their lands. Then at the end of the article was this:

> Ta'abata Qabit, the fifteen-year-old Sultan, has worked tirelessly to persuade the young people of his country, especially the girls, to take advantage of the new opportunities.